THE VOICE OF THE INTERROGATOR BOOMED

"Your name and rank."

Chase said nothing.

"I am awaiting your answer," the interrogator called.

"I have nothing to say," Chase replied.

There was the whirl of a hand-pedaled generator and electricity seared through his body. . . .

TORTURE CAN'T STOP *THE BOXER UNIT*

Books by Ned Cort

Boxer Unit — OSS #1: French Entrapment
Boxer Unit — OSS #2: Alpine Gambit
Boxer Unit — OSS #3: Operation Counter-Scorch

Published by
WARNER BOOKS

BOXER UNIT OSS

#3
OPERATION
COUNTER-SCORCH

NED CORT

WARNER BOOKS

A Warner Communications Company

In the Ligurian Sea, off the coast of northern Italy, a U.S. submarine rolled gently on the surface. It was night; the sky was overcast and the sea was calm. The only sound came from waves lapping the hull. Inland, hills flickered silently with lightning. On the bridge stood four men: the captain, two sailors, and a civilian with a Schmeisser machine pistol slung over his shoulder. The sailors were scanning the outer sea with binoculars for sign of enemy destroyers while the captain and the civilian were watching the shore for a signal from the agent who was to meet the boat's passengers. The submarine had brought a four-man team from the Office of Strategic Services, the World War II spy and sabotage agency, to go into Italy on a mission. They were the famous Group Boxer, the agency's multilingual rapid intervention unit. The civilian on the bridge was its leader. A tall, handsome blond with swept-back hair, his name was Nick Chase.

"There." He pointed as a torch flashed on the beach. He waited for the agent to repeat the signal. Short, long, short, short. The letter *L* in morse. "That's him."

"Acknowledge," the captain ordered one of the sailors. He walked to the voice pipe. "Boxers to the bridge, dinghy party on deck."

The submarine stirred to life. On deck the forehatch opened and sailors emerged with rubber dinghies, which they proceeded to inflate. From the conning tower hatch came the sound of feet climbing the ladder and the rest of the Boxers appeared. The first was a slim, sandy-haired man with wire-rimmed glasses, Jeff D'Arcy, the radio operator. He was followed by a brunet with a pencil-shaped mustache, Frank Kirilis, the demolition expert. Last came a swarthy individual with a curly beard, Chris Romer, the weapons instructor. Like Chase they were armed with Schmeissers—weapons for which ammunition was easily available in Italy—and wore trenchcoats over suits. The get up was part of their cover, an economic mission from neutral Argentina.

"Good luck with Counter-scorch," said the captain, shaking hands in turn.

They made their way down to the deck, where sailors were loading the dinghies with their luggage. Each Boxer had a suitcase containing his personal belongings. In addition there was a small one containing a radio. One of the sailors handed them their ammunition vests, which they put on. These were similar to hunting vests except that instead of pockets for cartridges there were pockets for magazines. Next he gave them inflatable life jackets, which they put over the vests. The end product was four fat men.

"Hey, this is what it must feel to be Laurel," said Kirilis, tapping his sides. "Or is it Hardy? I always get them mixed up."

"Hardy," said Romer.

The sky rumbled. D'Arcy glanced at the flickering hills and pocketed his glasses. "It's going to be touch and go."

"We'll make it," said Chase.

A look traveled between D'Arcy and Kirilis. Not that they questioned Chase's decision to go in, or his right to encourage them. It was his football coach tone of certainty, as if facing them were not the forces of nature but

6

the Yale Bulldogs and all that was required to win was a positive attitude. A tone slightly less certain, slightly more hopeful, would have been more appropriate. But that was Chase, positive to the extreme.

The sailors lowered the dinghies, the Boxers climbed in, and the crew pushed them off. Normally it was the job of the submarine to ferry a team to shore, but in view of the approaching storm the captain had asked them to ferry themselves. It would mean losing the dinghies, but he'd rather lose those than four crew men caught in the storm on the way back. The Boxers readily agreed to this, glad of an opportunity to repay the captain for the underwater champagne dinner he had thrown for them the previous night.

They paddled in silence with short, quick strokes, the way they had been trained to do, the boats joined by a rope so they wouldn't land too far apart. Every time the paddles dipped the water glowed, and when the paddles were withdrawn the dripping water also glowed. It was a natural phenomenon they had come across before, on a mission to Morocco, and it had something to do with the phosphoric content of the water. Although why it only glowed when stirred no one seemed to know, not even Kirilis, who should have known about such things, being a chemical engineer by profession.

On shore, the agent kept flashing his torch to give them a bearing. But the torch was moving away from them, to the left, telling them the current was taking them off course. They made no attempt to correct this; they would worry about meeting up with him later. Right now the important thing was to touch land, because if the storm caught them in deep water they would go down like stones. In addition to their ammunition belts they were weighted with gold dollars in money belts, money for raising a troop for their mission.

The rumbling in the sky grew louder and more frequent. A gust of wind, the first of the night, blew in their faces and they felt raindrops. The water turned choppy. Automatically they speeded up their paddling, the boat with Chase and D'Arcy leading, the one with Romer and Kirilis a few yards back to the right. Fifty yards to go. An ear-splitting bolt zig-zagged down in front of them and the wind picked up with a vengeance. On the beach trees swayed wildly and clouds of sand blew out to sea. Their paddling turned frantic, a race with the storm. Twenty-five yards to go. Twenty. Fifteen. And then it happened.

A wall of swelling water caught them from the back, lifting them into the air. The dinghies tipped and men and contents tumbled. With a foaming roar the lot spilled on the beach, all four stunned by the fall. Before any of them had time to react, the undertow receded, sucking them back into the sea, hands and faces scraping the sandy bottom. When they finally surfaced, coughing and spitting, they were almost back where the wave picked them up, feet touching ground, but up to their necks in water. Now it was every man for himself, man against nature, the crashing waves propelling them forward, the sea floor sliding from under their feet, pulling them backward. Ordinary mortals would have floundered, but these men were in tip-top shape. A lot of money had been spent keeping them that way, including teaching them how to get out of the sea in a storm: adopt a sitting position, walk with your feet, and breaststroke with your arms. Deafened by the crashing waves, blinded by sheets of rain, slipping, falling, they fought their way to land.

"Everyone okay?" Chase shouted. They stood around him in the flickering light, faces dripping with water. He saw them nod and exchange smiles. They were happy with the happiness that comes from cheating death. And they had done it in style. Not one man had lost his weapon.

"Look!" Romer shouted.

A woman was running towards them along the beach. They watched her speechlessly, for it was like something out of a film: the sand, the thunder, the lightning, and this young woman running barefoot towards them, one hand holding her shoes, the other a torch.

"Come on!" shouted Romer, the first to snap out of the trance.

They ran towards her.

"Are you the Boxers?" she shouted as they met. A good-looking woman with an intelligent face, she spoke English with just a touch of an Italian accent.

"Yes, that's us!" Chase shouted back. "Who are you?"

"I am Paola. I am your reception agent. I have a van in a wood near where I was. The current took you very far down. Luckily I could see you in the lightning. Are you all right? I thought you overturned."

"We did," Chase replied. "We lost all our luggage. But we're here."

"Can we go to the van?" she shouted over the thunder.

"Okay. You lead."

As she turned the Boxers exchanged glances. The last thing they had expected was that the agent would be a woman. And some woman, too. There was a presence about her that, combined with her looks—17 out of 20 on the Kirilis scale—made them all very keen to get to know her. She led them single file along the beach, their shoes sinking in the soggy sand, all of them leaning heavily against the wind, sheets of rain lashing their faces. All four felt the urge to offer their arm to her, but none did for fear of taking away from her glory. Eventually they came to a path and climbed a cliff at the top of which was a wood. In a clearing stood a Bianchi van. A curly-haired Italian with a boyish face jumped out. Paola introduced him as Cino. Like Paola, Cino spoke excellent English with barely a trace of an accent. The Boxers piled into the back and they drove off. For a couple of miles they went along a muddy path, then came out onto a highway. As the van picked up speed, Cino

9

said, "If we are stopped, I will close the partition and please don't make any noise. We have a police pass. The back door is locked."

The Bianchi sped northward, its headlights piercing the night. The lightning had passed but it was still raining. The road snaked past cliff-top villages and hills with terraced slopes on which olive trees grew. Liguria is famous for its olive oil. In the back of the van the Boxers dozed, lulled by the hum of the engines and the swish of the windshield wipers. All felt tired. It was well past midnight and the previous night, too, they had had little sleep. After the underwater champagne dinner they had put on a song fest for the crew, Romer on the submarine's guitar, D'Arcy on a harmonica. Speaking nine languages among them, having good voices and having picked up songs all over the world, the Boxers were always being asked to sing by crews transporting them. Their reputation as first-rate entertainers preceded them. The concert dragged on into the early hours with the sailors asking for more, especially for Romer's New England chanteys. He had a deep voice that lent itself to them. The others, too, made their contributions, Arab desert songs by D'Arcy—he spoke Arabic—Yugoslav partisan ballads by Kirilis, Italian love songs by Chase. It had been an exhausting night. All four were dying to go to bed.

"Carabinieri," Paolo warned.

"Close the partition," said Cino.

The back was plunged into darkness. The vehicle slowed down and came to a stop. Chase and Romer cocked an ear; both knew Italian. Romer's mother was Italian and Chase had gone to school in Italy when his father was in Rome serving as American ambassador.

"Good evening," they heard one of the Carabinieri say.

"Good evening," Cino replied. "A wet night."

10

"At least it's clearing." There was the rustle of paper. "Your destination?"

"La Spezia. Africa police headquarters. The lady is my secretary."

A pause. The sound of paper being folded. "Thank you. Good night."

"Good night."

They resumed their journey. The partition opened. "All is well," said Paola. "That was a Carabinieri roadblock."

"We are lucky they were not the Guardia," said Cino. "The Guardia would not have let us go so quickly."

"What do you mean?" asked Chase.

"The Guardia would have wanted to search. Anything to make us wait. The Guardia and the Italian Africa police don't like each other. They like annoying each other."

"What would you have done if they wanted to search?" Chase continued.

"We would have said no. They have no right to search Africa police cars, but they try. If you refuse enough they give up. They have no jurisdiction over the Africa police."

"Excuse me, but what is the Africa police?" asked Romer.

"The police of Italian colonies in Africa. When the Allies occupied Africa they returned to Italy with the army. They have their own uniforms and their own administration. The Guardia would like to take them over."

"And what is the Guardia?"

"The National Republican Guard. They are the official militia of the Republic. Half army, half police."

"Sorry, but which republic is this?" said Romer. He had always known Italy to be a monarchy.

Cino laughed. People always asked that. He explained. "When the Germans occupied Italy after the Armistice (when Italy quit the Axis and made a separate peace with the Allies), they created a puppet government and declared Italy a republic. The official title is the Italian

11

Social Republic. The capital is in Salo, in the north. Very few people outside Italy know about the Republic. It has not been in existence for very long."

They came to a fork in the road and Cino took the road to the right. "This is a mountain road," he explained, turning off the windshield wipers. It had stopped raining. "A little longer than the coastal road, but there is less chance we will meet patrols. We should be in La Spezia in about an hour."

The Bianchi wound its way into the mountains. Soon they were surrounded by towering peaks and heavy woods. It got colder, too. A road sign in German flashed by. Achtung! Banditengebeit. Attention! Bandit territory.

"Carabinieri," Paola warned.

"Again?" said Cino.

"An antipartisan operation must be on," said Paola.

The partition slid shut and once more the Boxers were plunged into darkness. The van slowed down and came to a stop.

"Your papers?" This time the tone was more curt. Chase and Romer strained their ears. The rustle of paper. A pause. "A Blackshirt, eh?"

"No, Italian Africa police."

"Italian Africa, Guardia, OVRA, what's the difference? You all come from the same sty. Get out!"

"Get out? Who do you think you are?"

"Autonomous partisans. Out, I said." There was the sound of the door being wrenched open. "Mario, give me a hand." The Bianchi swayed as a scuffle broke out. "Luigi, get the girl."

Boots thumped on the road; the other door was wrenched open. "Come, carina, out you get."

"Don't touch me!" Paola shouted.

In the back of the van, hands reached for the Schmeissers.

The van rocked, the Boxers bracing themselves against the sides. Two were pointing their weapons at the partition, two at the back door. Chase's mind whirled, going over courses of action open to them. One was to simply announce themselves. The partisans might accept them as bona fide OSS agents, he thought, or they might not. That is, if they were bona fide partisans themselves. Either way they would search them. And when they discovered the gold? Two OSS teams had already been lost that way, wiped out for the gold they carried. The alternative was to negotiate from strength with guns drawn. But how? The door was locked.

The scuffling continued. Paola was dragged from the cab, then Cino. But Paola went on fighting in the road. The Boxers could hear her spirited noises and Luigi's panting. There was the sound of a dress being torn.

"Bruto!" cried Paola.

Luigi cried in pain. "Cagna!" he swore. There was a slap.

"Carogna!" shouted Paola.

There were two more slaps and now it was Paola who cried in pain. They heard Luigi rasp pantingly, "Any more biting and I'll bash your head in."

In the van Chase's hand followed Romer's shoulder to the nape of his neck. He drew the head toward him, his mouth seeking Romer's ear, lips scraping the beard. He whispered for a moment and Romer moved catlike to the partition. They all wore rubber-soled shoes.

Outside Cino could be heard saying indignantly, "I demand to see your commanding officer."

There was a thud, Cino moaned, and a voice laughed. "That'll teach you not to be cheeky."

"Let me give the fascist swine a lesson," a new voice said. A fist thudded. Cino cried in pain.

"Basta!" called out the man who had stopped the van. "Luigi, drive the van off the road and go through it. Tino, you go with him. Luigi, meet us in the clearing."

There was the sound of running feet, and the van swayed as the two men got into the cab. The two doors

13

slammed shut and the van lurched forward. A hand tried to open the partition. Romer pushed on the knob with all his force.

"It's stuck," said a high-pitched voice that had to be Tino's. Luigi's voice they were familiar with from his swearing at Paola.

The Bianchi turned off the highway onto a forest trail. Chase repeated his cheek-to-cheek maneuver, this time with Kirilis. "Stand by the back door," Chase whispered. "Driver's side. Undo the sliding locks. When they try to open the door, we push it open."

The other tapped Chase's cheek to signify he understood. He slung the Schmeisser over his back, Russian cavalry style, and went to the door. Chase also put his weapon over his back and moved to the other half of the door, the one with the handle. If by any chance only one of the partisans came, he would block the handle until the other joined him. He wanted to catch both at once, otherwise one might escape.

The Bianchi turned off the trail, bumping over uneven ground. It came to a halt and both partisans descended. They came round the back and the handle turned. "Locked," said Luigi. "I'll get the key." They heard him walk to the cab and the engine was cut as he removed the keys from the ignition. He came back to the door. The key turned, the handle went down.

"Now!" hissed Chase.

Both halves of the door flew open, sending the partisans to the ground. Before they had time to recover, Chase and Kirilis were on top, hands over their mouths. Romer and D'Arcy followed on their heels. Each kneeled next to a prisoner and pressed the barrel of his weapon into the man's side. The whole operation was helped by the fact that the partisans had left the headlamps on, so there was some light to see by.

"Our guns have silencers, so we're not afraid of shoot-

14

ing," said Chase. "One squeak out of you, Luigi, and my friend here will pull the trigger."

At the sound of his name, Luigi's eyes, already wide, widened even further. Chase could tell there would be no squeak. It didn't surprise him. In the course of the war he had observed that men who went in for hitting women were seldom brave.

"Frank," said Chase in a loud whisper, "take your man into the van." When interrogating, it was wiser to separate prisoners. It lowered their morale. "And turn off the headlights."

With his hand still over the prisoner's mouth, Kirilis led Tino into the van. Romer slung his weapon over his shoulder and followed them inside. He sat on the floor next to Tino, took his hand, and put on a wrist hold.

"If you shout, I will do this," said Romer, applying a little pressure. The man winched. "I can break your wrist, so don't shout."

"I'll stand watch outside," said Kirilis, going out. He switched off the headlamps and walked to the trail. He selected a spot by a tree and knelt to listen.

The forest was silent, the only sound the occasional gust of wind through the pines and the dripping of water.

"Turn on your stomach, Luigi," Chase said finally. The man complied on the spot. "Your head sideways, so you can talk. Like that," he added, turning Luigi's head gently towards him. "Don't be afraid. We will not harm you, but we have to protect ourselves. On his stomach a man cannot shout."

"I won't shout," Luigi assured him.

"Good. Now then Luigi, we need some quick answers to a few questions." Chase looked up at D'Arcy. "Apply a little pressure, will you?" he said in English. The other jabbed his weapon in Luigi's side.

"I won't shout. Believe me."

The interview began. Where is the clearing? How many in the band? The name of the chief? Who is he?

15

What is the purpose of the operation? Luigi answered as fast as the questions came. A quarter of an hour later Chase had all the information he wanted.

He went to see Romer.

"They're going to kill Cino and Paola."

"I know, I've been talking to this guy as well. We'll have to hurry."

"We have a bit of time. They'll have to dig graves."

"You have a plan?"

"Try and surprise them. Free Cino and Paola. After that, we'll have to play it by ear. My man will lead us."

"What about this guy? What do we do with him?"

"Any way of incapacitating him? We can't take both. Too risky."

"There's nothing to tie him with and the doors are too flimsy to hold him. A good kick and he could be out."

Chase paused to consider the alternatives. There weren't any. "Okay, delete him. Where do you want to do it?"

"In here will be fine."

"We'll wait for you by the trail," said Chase. He went out, shutting the door behind him. His foot stepped on something—the car keys. He gave them to D'Arcy, the team's getaway driver.

A little later something bumped inside the van and the vehicle swayed. A throat gurgled and feet drummed the floor. After a period of silence, the door opened and Romer emerged, pulling a body by the jacket collar. He dragged it along the ground to a clump of bushes and dumped it. He set out for the trail.

In a clearing lit by flaming torches Cino and Paola were digging their grave watched by two lines of men. The firing squad. They stood feet apart with rifles by their side in a stance drill sergeants call stand easy. The men were young and dressed in a variety of clothes: army

16

uniform, city suits, hiking clothes, and combinations. They were factory workers, farm hands, ex-soldiers, fishermen, students, men out of work. All had fled their homes down in the valleys for the safety of the mountains to avoid labor conscription or military service. In the mountains they had been recruited by Lupo, the Wolf.

An army deserter turned bandit, Lupo had been a small-time outlaw until the Armistice changed his fortunes. Until the Armistice Italy was united behind the Duce, and for Italians to kill each other was a crime. The Armistice created a civil war situation where this became a patriotic act, provided of course it was done under one of two banners, Fascist or anti-Fascist. Lupo chose the later because it offered a faster road to rehabilitation. The fascist police would throw him in jail, or perhaps shoot him. The anti-Fascist partisans, on the other hand, might declare him a hero, even though for the moment they did not want to talk to him. He had made overtures for affiliation to Justice and Liberty, the Group of Patriotic Action, the Green Flame, all highly respected organizations receiving money and arms from the Allies, but none would have him. A bandit-turned-partisan whose banda was no more than sixty men was a nobody. Lupo set about to become somebody. The first thing was to increase his numbers. The arrival of the Boxers coincided with his campaign of recruitment, *permanent* recruitment. The bane of the partisan movement in Italy was desertions. All kinds of people signed up to be partisans only to discover that the life wasn't for them, and they went home. Authorities tended to turn a blind eye, writing off their partisan sojourn as a youthful transgression. Unless a man had been involved in highly criminal activity, he had little to worry about. Lupo instituted the executions to make sure he had lots to worry about. Every recruit was made to take part in the murder of a civilian Fascist, kidnapped at random. So that the recruit's participation would not escape unnoticed, villagers from mountain

17

hamlets were pressed into acting as torch holders and be witnesses. By this method Lupo had increased the size of his banda to nearly two hundred men. They were in his main hideout on the other side of a range. For this operation he had brought only the latest recruits and a few oldtimers to lead them.

"I counted seventeen," Romer whispered. He had just rejoined the others after a reconnaissance of the clearing. "Eleven in the execution squad and six older types. They look like NCOs."

"Is Lupo among them?" asked Chase.

Romer nodded. "I recognized him from Luigi's description." In an afterthought, he added, "Bless his soul." After Luigi had led them to the clearing, he had gone the way of Tino. To have had him around would have been taking too much of a risk.

"Give us the layout," said Chase. "Who's where?"

"On the north side of the clearing, Cino and Paola are digging a grave. On the southern is the firing squad. The NCOs are standing in a group with Lupo in the west. There are about ten villagers, mainly women holding torches. They're all round."

Chase paused to think. "Okay," he said finally. "Here is what we do." He explained the plan.

They split up into pairs. Romer and Kirilis made their way to the eastern edge. Chase and D'Arcy crawled to the northern. That way if a fire fight broke out and they had to retreat, they would be backing towards the Bianchi. Before setting out they unscrewed the silencers. If there was a fire fight, the noise of their machine pistols would be to their advantage, unsettling the opposition, who were armed only with rifles.

By the time the Boxers were in position Cino and Paola were up to their waists in the grave, still digging. Both were taking their time. The firing squad watched them in silence. So did the villagers. But the men Romer called the NCOs chatted away gaily. Lupo was with them, a stocky man with a mustache in the uniform of a Carabinieri brigadier. Two others were also in Carabinieri uniforms, the rest in paramilitary clothes. One wore a suit topped by an Italian navy cap.

"Eh, Cino, put a spurt on, will you?" shouted one of the NCOs, a short man in a helmet. "Saint Peter is waiting." There were guffaws from the others.

In the trench Paola paused to straighten her back, her dress torn from the scuffle with Luigi.

"You, too, carina," said the same man, playing to his colleagues. "We haven't got all night."

"Go to the devil," Paola retorted.

As she bent and resumed digging, Chase and D'Arcy rose behind their respective trees. They had to get up to have a clear field of fire. The earth mound by the grave obstructed it. Chase took a deep breath and shouted in English, "Cino, Paola, get down so we can fire over you!" Then switching to Italian, he shouted, "Everybody hands up! German police. You're surrounded." The partisans scorned Italian police, but German police they feared.

Hardly had the words left his mouth than there was a burst of Schmeisser fire from Romer's side, and a man cried in pain. Women screamed, torches fell to the ground, and there was a general stampede. Chase and D'Arcy stepped from behind the trees and fired over heads, the object of the exercise being not to kill but to make them run in the desired direction.

The sound of running feet gave way to the sizzle of torches burning in the wet grass. Chase peered from behind his tree. By the light of the torches he saw three shapes on the ground. One stirred, moaned, and fell still. Chase withdrew his head and listened. The forest was silent, the only sound moving branches and dripping water. But he wasn't going to take chances.

"Cino, Paola, are you safe?" he called. "Answer me."

"What do you want us to do?" Cino cried from the bottom of the trench.

"When I say go, crawl on your hands and knees towards me. On your hands and knees," he repeated, "so I can fire over your heads. I will be firing over your heads. Go!" He opened fire, spraying the far side with short bursts, covering fire in case any of Lupo's people stayed behind to pull a fast one. As Chase's magazine ran out, D'Arcy took over, firing until Cino and Paola reached them.

"Gesù Bambino," Paola sighed, panting. "I thought we were lost."

"Join hands," Chase ordered, taking hers. "You, too, Cino." To the others he shouted, "Chris, Frank, take over!"

Romer and Kirilis opened up with their weapons to cover Chase's retreat, firing in various directions. Then they too pulled out, catching up with the others on the way. The six of them ran for the Bianchi.

When they got to it, Chase led Paola and Cino into the back and closed the door. D'Arcy got in behind the wheel, Romer next to him, and Kirilis hanging on the running board on D'Arcy's side. The engine burst to life and headlamps lit up the night. With Kirilis guiding, D'Arcy backed the van into the trail, turned it, and hit the gas.

They shot out of the forest and, tires screaming, turned into the highway. A kilometer down the road D'Arcy stopped and everyone changed places, going back to the earlier seating arrangement, the Boxers in the back, Cino and Paola in front.

"Why did you open fire?" Chase asked as the van moved off.

"Lupo and one of the NCOs raised their rifles at you," said Romer.

"Was Lupo hit?"

"Yes, he fell."

The Bianchi sped towards La Spezia.

The first thing that struck them about the town were the lights. The streetlamps were on, there were lights in the harbor, lights in the industrial section, lights blazing from office buildings. You would have thought the war was over.

"Don't they believe in blackouts here?" asked Romer.

"Blackouts are a thing of the past," replied Cino. "Everyone knows the Allies now are more interested in preserving than in destroying."

They passed a large building with German soldiers in guard booths and a swastika flying from the balcony. It, too, was ablaze with lights.

"What's in there?" asked Chase.

"Headquarters of the Fourth Sapper Battalion," replied Cino, "the ones installing the demolition charges."

They drove through the town, its deserted streets shining from the rain. The Bianchi climbed a hill and pulled up outside a villa.

"Your residence, gentlemen," announced Paola.

They followed her inside a large house with marble floors and fans on the roof, full of plants and flowers. It had all the modern conveniences from shower to telephone.

"If you are hungry, there is food in the kitchen," said Paola. "There is bread, and there are eggs, and there is cheese. The milk is in the icebox."

"Do we have you to thank for this?" asked Chase.

"Only for the food and the flowers," said Paola. "The rest is Henrik's. He rented the villa."

"Thank you for the food and the flowers," said Chase, inclining his head. "Especially the flowers."

Paola gave him an appreciative look and acknowledged the thanks with a similar gesture. It was obvious she was taken by this man who appreciated her thoughtfulness.

"Where is Henrik?" asked Chase.

21

"He was called back to Genoa," Paola replied, "which is why he sent us to meet you. He will be back this morning." The back of her hand went up to her forehead as if she had just thought of something. "You will need clothes, won't you?" she said, surveying their raincoats muddied from crawling in the forest.

"Yes, and toiletries," said Chase.

"I will speak to Henrik. He will get you some. In the meantime, tonight," she mimicked tooth brushing, "with your finger."

A schoolmistress, Chase thought. He was willing to bet she was a schoolmistress. She had the manner. Now children, this is what you do when you don't have a toothbrush.

She led them into the bathroom and showed them how to operate the showers—if you moved the lever in the wrong direction you could scald yourself—showed them where the towels were, where the iron and the ironing board were kept, and how to fix the toilet, which tended to stick when flushed and make an annoying noise. A thorough woman.

"I think that is all," she said finally. "Well, good night," she added, shaking their hands. "And once again, thank you for saving our lives."

They were awakened by the sound of mandolins interspersed with the ringing of the front door bell. The mandolins came from the hotel next door, whose band was practicing in the hotel's garden. The ringing was from Henrik Szendroy. An elegant individual with the shiniest pair of brogues outside a bootcamp, he had come with two men carrying suitcases. Szendroy was a Hungarian count married to a wealthy American woman. The couple had settled in Genoa in the thirties, where they amused themselves dealing in art. When the war broke out they took on a sideline: intelligence. Both were on the OSS

22

payroll as the agency's agents-in-residence on the Italian Riviera.

The suitcase contained toiletries and clothes for the Boxers. Not knowing the Boxers' measurements, he had brought the shop to the villa, the way things were done in the good old days in Budapest. The men with him were the employees of a local menswear shop. While they were being outfited, Szendroy ordered breakfast from the hotel. It arrived on trays carried by waiters. They had it on the balcony of the villa.

It was a glorious day with blue skies and a light breeze. To their left lay the port, to the right in the hills the hydro station. The oil refinery and petrochemical plants were on a plain on the other side of town, their tall stacks issuing white vapor or flickering flames. Beyond them lay an industrial park, Italy's first.

"Hell! It's huge," said Kirilis.

"Every one of those plants," said Szendroy, "is either mined or will be. The same applies to the port installations. The hydroelectric station, too, is mined. And they will probably mine the dam as well."

"Are they doing this all over Italy?" asked Romer.

"The orders from Berlin are for every major industrial installation in the north to be destroyed. Of course some commanders are ignoring them. In La Spezia, unfortunately, it's the reverse—the Germans are being very thorough. We had a visit from a Gouleiter to make sure Berlin's orders are carried out."

"Oh?" said Chase.

"A settling of scores is involved. The Führer is determined that Kramer will suffer. When he came to power, Kramer's German subsidiary was one of the few companies that refused to contribute to Nazi party funds."

"Sorry, but who is Kramer?" asked Romer.

"Kramer Industries. A large multinational corporation specializing in petrochemicals. They are the ones who developed La Spezia. Many of those plants are owned by

23

Kramer. They also own the hydroelectric station and have shares in the company that operates the port. You must know Jim Russel, no? He is one of Kramer's directors."

The Boxers exchanged glances. Russel was deputy director of the OSS. So that's why London was so keen to get them going with Counter-scorch. They had wondered about that. The previous week they had been parachuted into Belgium to steal plans of a new antitank weapon being made by the Fabrique Nationale. The day after their arrival they received a message cancelling the mission and ordering them to stand by for exfiltration by Lysanders. It was the first time such a thing had happened, a mission cancelled midway through.

Szendroy smiled knowingly. "Yes, it is not every company that can call on the OSS to protect it from Hitler's scorched earth policy, no?"

"Indeed," said D'Arcy.

"Two days after they heard of Hitler's plans, Kramer offered Russel a directorship. That is what I call being on the ball." It was the sort of expression one did not expect from a Hungarian count, but Szendroy was an Americanized count. He had lived most of his life in the States.

"Bruce Hopkins told me you would give us a list of priorities," said Chase.

"My friends, to Mister Kramer and Mister Russel the whole of La Spezia is a priority."

"We realize that," Kirilis broke in, "but we still must have an idea of where we should begin counter-scorching. I mean, do we start on the port facilities or the hydro station? The enemy might decide to begin scorching in a couple of days. We can't counter-scorch the whole town in two days."

"Frank is our demolition and antidemolition expert," explained Chase.

"Very well, I see your point. First priority, the hydro

24

station, second the refinery and the petrochemical plants, third the harbor installations, last the industrial park."

Kirilis looked at Chase. "Offhand I would say we will need at least a thousand men."

"Manpower should present no problem," Szendroy assured them. "The hills around La Spezia are full of men, most of them starving: partisans, deserters, escaped POWs, people running from labor conscription or military service."

"Yes, we know, we met some on our way here," said D'Arcy.

"I heard about that. Paola told me. Incidentally, how do you find my two recruits?" he asked proudly.

"Who are they?" asked Chase.

"The children of a friend, a brewer from Genoa. They are brother and sister. Cino works as an engineer for the harbor board and Paola runs an orphanage. Paola is a lawyer by profession but she gave it up. Personally, I find her the more interesting of the two."

Kirilis smiled. "So do we."

"Well, you won't have any competition from me," said Szendroy, returning the smile. "Twenty years ago," he sighed, "perhaps. But to come back to manpower, I think the wisest thing for you to do would be to discuss this with Piero-Piero. He is the comandante of the Communist partisans in this area. The Communists are the only people worth talking to, the only ones who are organized. The others are bandits or so small they would be no use to you. I spoke to Piero-Piero yesterday and even made a tentative arrangement for you to meet this afternoon. I suggest you call me at one at my office to check." Szendroy took out a visiting card from his wallet and handed it to Chase. "Call me at one."

"Is there any possibility of hiring a car?" asked Chase. "We'd like to take a tour of the installations and get the layout of the town."

"You don't need to rent a car," said Szendroy. "There's

25

an Aprilia in the garage for your use." He handed Chase a set of keys. "There are gasoline coupons in the glove compartment and a map." He glanced at his watch. "I must rush. I have an appointment with a rich art buyer."

"Another thing," said Chase. "We lost our radio in the sea."

"Paola told me. No problem. I will lend you mine. I will send it with Cino or Paola." He surveyed the dishes. "When you have finished call the hotel to clear this. Don't worry about security. The hotel owner is in the resistance."

After Szendroy left, D'Arcy said, "There's an operator if ever I saw one. Art dealer, OSS agent, married into money, and I wouldn't be surprised if he turns out to be working for Kramer on top of it."

"Don't knock him, Jeff," said Chase. "He could have put us up in a rooming house and we'd be eating polenta. Instead, we've got ourselves a small palazzo."

"With a house full of nurses at the back," Romer added.

"What's this?" asked Kirilis.

"One of the clothing salesmen told me. Our back garden borders on a hospital compound. The nearest building to us is a nurses' home. Apparently several hundred nurses live there."

Kirilis turned to Chase. "What do you say, Comandante, isn't a reconnaissance in order?"

Chase smiled, amused by Lothario's enthusiasm. "Later. Let's get those factories reconnoitered first."

They first toured the town. The center had charm: narrow streets with quaint architecture, squares with monuments and fountains, trees, gardens, tourists. Then they headed for the suburbs. Rows of long apartment houses of almost barracklike severity. Wide streets. Vacant lots overgrown with weeds awaiting sale by land speculators. Pasty-faced factory workers. Trucks, bicycles. Urchins. The Boxers had the impression of driving through two different towns,

26

a high-class resort on the coast, a grimy industrial town in the interior.

They drove past the oil refinery which processed crude from Rumania now that Libya, an Italian colony, was in Allied hands. They went by the petrochemical plants, which produced synthetic rubber, industrial alcohol, ethylene, benzine, and other petroleum derivatives. They toured the industrial park where factories used the derivatives for the manufacture of tires, ink, aspirins, glues, paints, anesthetic, antifreeze.

Twice they were stopped by patrols of the Carabinieri and on each occasion their Argentinian passports worked like magic. They were smiled at and waved on.

"How come Argentinians are so popular in Italy?" asked Kirilis from the back.

"Argentina is a second Italy," replied Chase. He sat in front next to D'Arcy, who was driving. "At least a third of the population is of Italian origin. And the government is pro-Axis."

"Have you been to Argentina?" asked Romer.

"Yes, while I was working on Wall Street. A lot of our clients came from Argentina. I had to make periodic trips down there. A very rich country."

"Where to now?" asked D'Arcy. They had reached the end of the industrial park.

"The power station," said Chase. He turned to Romer. "Let's have the guns."

"Mind your feet," said Romer to Kirilis. He bent down and opened a secret compartment under the seat. He brought out their Schmeissers and passed them out.

"Let's hope we don't get stopped by the Carabinieri again," said D'Arcy, covering his weapon with a raincoat. "If they find these . . ."

"I'd rather risk a shootout with the Carabinieri than be murdered by bandits," said Chase.

The weapons were a departure from their routine. The usual procedure when reconnoitering a target was to do it unarmed so as to avoid incriminating evidence if they were caught in a spot control. What made them take their machine pistols on this reconnaissance was Szendroy's parting advice. If they went out of town, even to the power station, they should go armed. The danger of being attacked by bandits outweighed the danger of being stopped by a patrol. The hills were rife with outlaws.

It took them an hour to reach the dam. It lay astride the River Astri, forming a lake. From the side of the lake ten rows of penstocks ran down the mountain, carrying water to the turbine generators in the station below. Next to the station stood the transformers, from which sagging power lines held up by transmission towers carried the electricity to the coast.

A lookout had been built for people to contemplate the dam and that's where they parked their car. They took their raincoat-wrapped weapons with them and sat down on a bench, all but D'Arcy, who lay down on the grassy slope, face up to the sun. It was a lovely day: the sun hot, the air cool. While D'Arcy sunbathed, the others contemplated the dam and the guard booths that flanked it.

"This is the way to fight a war," said D'Arcy, sighing with pleasure. "Beats Wallonia."

"You can say that again," said Kirilis. In Beligum, it had been cold and foggy.

"Nick?" said D'Arcy.

"What?"

"Can't you get us a mission in the South Sea Islands? Tahiti, for instance. I've always had the urge to go there. Now's the time to do it, before the war ends and the agency is disbanded." D'Arcy spreadeagled and sighed. "I'll have great difficulty getting used to paying for my travels again."

"Poor Jeff," said Romer.

"What do you say, Nick?" D'Arcy went on. "There must be a way to swing a mission down there. Or maybe

28

Papua. Another place I've always had the urge to visit, Papua. Anyway, somewhere exotic. I'm tired of the Northern Hemisphere."

"Jeff, have you been drinking?" asked Romer.

"It's the mountain air," said Kirilis.

"No, I haven't been drinking," said D'Arcy. "I am simply happy."

Chase turned to Kirilis. "Are there wires along that dam wall or is it my imagination?"

"They've mined it, all right."

"There will be an awful lot of swimming down in La Spezia if that dam goes," D'Arcy mused.

They fell silent, listening to the wind whistling through the grass. Somewhere a bell tinkled and a goat bleated. Then their attention was caught by the noise of a Savoia-Marchetti dropping leaflets over the hills on the other side of the river.

"I wonder what that's about?" said Kirilis.

As if in answer, the bomber broke out of its pattern, flew towards them, and released a shower of paper over their heads. It was obviously done as a joke, for as he passed the pilot dipped his wings. The leaflets floated to the ground and they all took one.

"In what language is this?" said D'Arcy, holding up his leaflet.

"Polish," said Romer, who had picked up a similar pamphlet. He spoke the language.

"Mine is in French," said Chase.

"And mine in Italian," said Kirilis. He threw it away and took another. "Hey, this one is in English."

"Read it," said D'Arcy.

The other read aloud: " 'War prisoners who have evaded from concentration camps. Foreigners who are wandering in the impervious regions of Italy. Remember! The Italian Army has been thoroughly reorganized and you will soon discover what a frightful fate is hanging over

29

your heads.' Hey, how do you like that? A frightful fate is hanging on our heads."

"Keep going," said Chase impatiently.

" 'Should you be caught while in possession of arms, or should you have joined a gang of partisans, you will be considered franc-tireurs and as such you will be tried in accordance with the laws of war. Why, then, will you still put up with hunger, defy danger and suffer all sort of discomforts? Why should you prolong your suffering for the sake of what is a hopeless cause?' " Kirilis' tone took on a declamatory style. " 'Surrender to the Italian military authorities who will treat you as well as they did formerly and will again recognize you as war prisoners. Only following this course will you be able to see again your Fatherland and the dear ones who are anxiously awaiting your return home.' Then there's a line at the bottom, but it's in Italian." He showed it to Chase.

"Printed in Italian, English, French, and Polish," Chase translated.

"Why Polish?" asked Kirilis.

"There's a Polish Corps with the Eighth Army," said Romer.

"Let's go," said Chase, rising. "We still have to do the harbor."

They got back inside the car and headed back.

Halfway down they came face to face with a German convoy. It was led by an armored car, armed with a cannon. The narrow road and bordering cliffs prevented passing, so D'Arcy backed the Aprilia several hundred yards to a stretch of flat ground. He drove off the road and they watched the convoy go by. The armored car was followed by a Kübelwagen, the German version of a jeep. An officer sat next to the driver and at the back a soldier leaned against a mounted machine gun. Next came a police van with grilled windows, followed by two trucks with troops. As the van passed, a crumpled piece of paper was pushed through the grills. It was obviously a message and it fell to the ground without the escort noticing it. When the convoy had passed, the Boxers retrieved the paper. On one side was a dated message, partly in Italian, partly in English. In Italian it said, "Give this note to the first Allied officer you meet. He will reward you." In English it continued, "En route to La Spezia lime quarry to be executed. Survivors of Force 9. Avenge us!" On the reverse were twenty-two names with their rank and serial number. One look at the serials told the Boxers the men in the van were Americans.

There was a long silence as the Boxers weighed the pros and cons on what no one had mentioned but what was on everyone's mind. The buzz of a fly on the inside of the windshield only underlined it. D'Arcy switched off the engine.

"Well?" he said. "Left or right?"

"I wonder what Force Nine stands for?" said Kirilis.

"Probably a Special Force unit," said Chase.

"On a commando raid that failed," suggested Romer.

"Why would they execute them?" asked Kirilis.

"Any number of reasons," said D'Arcy. He was the team's psychowarfare expert. "Maybe they weren't in uniform. Or the Germans hope that by executing them they will deter future raids. Hitler has issued special orders about the treatment of commandos. Or maybe they're shooting them in reprisal for something we did. Don't forget our side are not angels, either."

There was another long silence.

"Okay, so what do we do?" said Chase.

"I vote we go left," said Romer.

Chase looked questioningly at D'Arcy.

"We'll be jeopardizing Counter-scorch," replied the other. "If Counter-scorch fails because of this, Bruce will throw the book at us. We all know the orders. Counter-scorch and nothing else. Bruce was very explicit about that."

"Bruce, Bruce, screw Bruce!" Kirilis burst out. "There

are the people we're fighting this war for," he said, jabbing his finger in the direction of the convoy. "Defending a millionaire's interests—"

"Let Jeff finish," said Chase angrily.

"A courtmartial will make mincemeat of us. Five years in the cooler, minimum."

"The war will be over before then," Kirilis retorted. "You said so yourself."

D'Arcy's eyes went to the rearview mirror. "And what makes you think that will change things? You think the Army is going to release us because the war is over? They operate stockades in peacetime, too."

"Are you telling me you're not prepared to sacrifice five years of your freedom to save the lives of twenty-two men?"

"Now that's a silly thing to say, Frank." Chase reprimanded him.

D'Arcy was the group's Devil's Advocate. As the least emotional of the four, he was expected to give the opposite point of view, no matter how unpalatable. It was a role that made him vulnerable to accusations of cynicism, callousness. By common consensus, they never took advantage. Now Kirilis had broken the rule by adopting a holier-than-thou attitude. Not only was the remark a blow under the belt, it was a blow at the very structure of the group.

"I'm sorry Jeff," said Kirilis, trying to repair the damage. "I shouldn't have said that."

"Forget it," said D'Arcy. Emotional outbursts from Kirilis were nothing new. He was by far the most emotional of the lot, except—as D'Arcy was fond of remarking—when blowing things up. Then he was as cool as a cucumber. Another natural phenomenon, unexplainable like that glowing water. In any case, as different as the two were emotionally, there was a bond between them that seemed to cushion their differences. The bond was their Greek blood, D'Arcy through his Greek mother, Kirilis through his Greek father.

"So what is it, Jeff?" asked Chase. If they were going to attempt rescuing those prisoners, it was time to get going.

"I'm for it."

"Okay, left," said Chase.

The surrounding cliffs echoed to the pounding of hammers as soldiers drove piles into the ground. The Boxers observed them from behind rocks atop a hill. They had arrived unnoticed, stopping before the last bend in the road, and had cut across the hillside on foot. The hill sloped to a road on the side of which were parked the armored car, the Kübelwagen, and one of the trucks. From the road the ground sloped to a flat stretch on which the soldiers were erecting the execution posts. The prison van and one of the trucks, probably the one that carried the piles, stood nearby. The escorting force was on the flat, except for five men who were on the road with the vehicles. They included the Kübelwagen machine gunner, still leaning on his weapon, and the driver of the armored car, sitting on the edge of the turret.

"I count thirty-one in all," said Romer.

Chase motioned them to get down. "Okay, so how do we incapacitate thirty-one men? Anybody got ideas?"

"We have to capture the Puma," said Romer.

"Right," said D'Arcy. "Without that armored car we don't stand a chance."

"The driver's in the turret, so we can't rush them," said Romer. "It would take him a second to duck and close the hatch."

Kirilis said, "How about you picking off the driver?"

Romer, the team's marksman, shook his head. "Not with a Schmeisser. Too far. I'd need a sniper's rifle."

"Suppose we walked up to them, pretending we are

33

Germans," Kirilis suggested. Chase spoke German fluently.

"The moment they see our weapons they'll have the Spandau trained on us," said Chase. "They'll alert the rest as well."

"Two of us could go unarmed. The other two could carry the weapons in raincoats."

"Then we can't be Germans," said Chase. "Can you see Germans wandering about these hills unarmed?"

"Why don't we drive in?" suggested D'Arcy.

There was a pause, accompanied by an exchange of glances. That sounded most realistic. "Okay, let's try that," said Chase. They discussed who would do what, then ran to their car.

The first batch of prisoners was being led from the van when the Aprilia drew up by the Kübelwagen. At its approach, the gunner swung his weapon around so that it faced them, although he didn't actually point it at them. The others surveyed the arrivals with curiosity.

"Sicherheitsdienst," Chase announced through the lowered windows. The tone was that of a bored policeman, the look suspicious. Policemen were always suspicious. "Who's in charge here?" Chase scowled. Everything about him said he was a nasty policeman. Chase had discovered that while people tended to be wary of friendly strangers, doubting their motives, they never doubted you if you were unpleasant.

"The lieutenant is on the execution ground," answered one of the soldiers by the truck, a young man.

"Ask him to come up," said Chase. "Tell him Hauptsturmführer von Jäger wants to talk to him."

"Jawohl, Herr Hauptsturmführer," said the soldier, snapping to atention. A captain of the SS secret police was someone you jumped for. He ran down the slope.

Chase gave a bored sigh and opened the door. Wearily he stepped out of the car, Schmeisser in hand, minus the silencer so as not to attract attention. A silencer was a curio. He slung the weapon over his shoulder and, hands

34

on hips, surveyed the goings-on below. The prisoners were being tied to the stakes. And they *were* in uniform. Out of the corner of his eye he saw the gunner staring at him. Chase met his gaze. "Turn that thing round, will you? It makes me nervous."

A half-amused, half-mocking expression crossed the gunner's face, then together with the gun, he turned his back on Chase. The slow way in which he turned, the air with which he did it, the final stance was sheer insolence. But it was experienced insolence, enough to annoy but not enough to latch on to. A professional soldier. Romer would have to be quick, Chase told himself.

Chase turned his attention to the driver of the Puma. "Where is the commander of your car?" he asked.

"Lieutenant Ehrlich is with Lieutenant Monter," the other replied, not bothering to explain who Lieutenant Monter was or where he was, then looked away in a manner that said he had no time for Chase. He was siding with the gunner.

The men's attitude pleased Chase. It showed they believed him to be an SS policeman. Wehrmacht troops, especially older men as both the gunner and driver were, were often sullen towards the SS, especially to SS men from the Sicherheitsdienst, who combined all the nasty qualities of military policemen and Nazi party fanatics. The young ones tended to be more friendly. Some even admired the SS, considering them Germany's finest soldiers.

On the execution ground the soldier from the road was reporting to an officer who kept glancing in Chase's direction. The officer made a gesture to say he was coming and carried on talking to a group of men holding blindfolds. The soldier headed back for the road.

"Sturmführer Römer," Chase threw over his shoulder. "Come see the execution. Driver, park the car to the side."

Romer joined Chase while D'Arcy drove the car to the

other side of the road, away from the vehicles. They didn't want to damage the Aprilia in the shootout. Below, soldiers were now blindfolding the prisoners. The soldier returned.

"Lieutenant Monter said he will come up after the first execution."

"Thank you."

The soldier turned to watch the execution. The eyes of all of the men on the road were on the ground below, where the firing squad was forming ranks. Chase looked at Romer, their eyes met, and he nodded. Casually they unslung their Schmeissers and, aiming from the hip, swiveled outward, Romer going for the gunner, Chase for the driver. Two bursts of gunfire rent the air. The gunner toppled out of the Kübelwagen, the driver half rose and slid inside the turret. Another burst killed the soldier who had gone with the message, another killed one of the drivers, while the fifth dived and rolled down the slope.

D'Arcy and Kirilis leaped out of the Aprilia, Kirilis racing for the Spandau, D'Arcy for the armored car. Kirilis jumped into the Kübelwagen and the Spandau burst to life, its hammerlike bark echoing between the cliffs, geysers of dirt rising from where the bullets landed. The firing squad threw itself to the ground. On top of the armored car Chase and D'Arcy struggled with the body of the driver, whose foot was stuck inside. The body was blocking the hatch. Bullets began flying past them as soldiers below returned the fire, some clanging against the car's armor and ricocheting with the sound of a pulled guitar string.

"Keep them pinned!" Chase shouted.

The cliffs resounded to the sound of gunfire, Kirilis firing away, Romer feeding the ammunition belt. On top of the Puma Chase and D'Arcy struggled with the body. Finally it gave. They threw it over the side and went down the hatch, D'Arcy first, for he would be driving. Chase pulled the hatch cover down after him, the Puma's engine

36

came to life, and the car shot forward down the slope towards the line of execution posts. Just before they got to it, D'Arcy turned left. Now the blindfolded men were on their right and the enemy on the left.

Halfway down the line, D'Arcy brought the car to a stop. Chase swiveled the turret so the cannon pointed at the slope. That's why they had performed this maneuver, agreed upon earlier, so they would be firing *away* from their own; also, to prevent the enemy from retreating to the line of stakes and using the prisoners as a shield. Chase aimed and pressed the firing pedal. The Puma shuddered as the cannon blazed. A fountain of earth rose on the slope. A body cartwheeled in the air.

D'Arcy switched seats and opened up with the car's machine gun. Bullets churned the ground. To their right another machine gun opened fire, the Spandau. Romer had driven the Kübelwagen down too and parked next to the Puma. On the slope the enemy soldiers lay behind rocks and boulders, not daring to stick a head out, pinned by the machine gun fire, but alive. If the machine guns couldn't reach them, however, the cannon could.

The turret swiveled to the right. Chase aimed for a spot between two boulders. He pressed the foot pedal and the cannon fired. The projectile exploded in a fountain of red and orange, earth and rock, and arms and legs. Chase reloaded and swiveled the turret again, looking for a likely hiding place. The foot pedal came down, the Puma shuddered. Boom! Another flash, another fountain. Chase reloaded. The turret swiveled, searching.

"White flag, eleven o'clock." He heard D'Arcy on the intercom.

Chase swiveled the turret to eleven o'clock. A hand was waving a white handkerchief from behind a boulder. "Keep them covered," he said into the intercom. He opened the hatch and stuck his head out. "Cease fire!" he shouted to Kirilis. But they had seen the handkerchief too and had stopped shooting. Chase cocked the machine

37

gun on the outside of the turret and pointed it towards the slope. "Chris, Frank, free the prisoners. I'll cover you."

From behind a blindfolded man cried out, "Sweet Mary, Jesus, Americans!"

"Jeff," said Chase on the intercom. "Drive up to them slowly. I'm manning the top machine gun."

The Puma moved forward. A hundred yards from the rocks and boulders, Chase ordered D'Arcy to stop. In German he shouted, "All prisoners gather by the rock with the bushes on your right. Hands up and hurry up!"

From behind the boulders men rose, hands held high. "The rock with the bushes to your right," Chase repeated. "Schnell!" He watched the soldiers, finger on the firing button.

A major from the prisoner van came running up. "Major Ogle of Force Nine," he said, climbing on the car and offering his hand. "Boy, are we glad to see you."

"Why were they executing you?"

"We killed some of their men, trying to break out of prison. We were captured last week while attacking coastal guns near Genoa. Are you with the partisans?"

"Sort of," said Chase. "Schnell! Schnell!" he called to the Germans. He turned to the major. "Get your men to collect the weapons. Also, if they see any enemy alive they should drag them to those rocks with the bushes."

"Will do," said the major, running off.

The Kübelwagen with Romer and Kirilis pulled up by the Puma's side. "What next?" asked Romer.

"The usual," said Chase. He glanced to his right. The rescued Americans were between the rocks stripping the dead of ammunition belts and collecting weapons. The German prisoners were assembled, some holding up wounded comrades. "Form ranks," Chase ordered in German. "Four abreast, facing me."

The prisoners formed four ranks. There were seventeen of them. The officer commanding the escort—the other lieutenant had been killed—took his place at the head of the formation. At that moment the Force Nine major came up.

"What are you going to do with them?" he asked.

"Ready, Frank?" said Chase, ignoring the major.

"Ready."

They opened fire simultaneously. Bullets ripped into the mass of humanity, tearing at flesh and limb. Others thudded into the rock, ricocheting into the air. The bodies crumpled one after another until all lay in a heap, but still the machine guns hammered away. Too often men survived by falling and pretending to be dead.

"Ceasefire," called Chase, finally.

The major stared at Chase. "Was that really necessary?"

"They were about to do the same thing to you, Major," Chase replied.

"Yes, but we're Americans, not Nazis."

Chase considered this in silence. "That's true, Major." He nodded thoughtfully. "I guess I hadn't thought of it." He was in no mood for explanations. If they had let those prisoners go—that was the only alternative—the prisoners could have provided the Gestapo with useful information: four Americans driving an Aprilia, two blond, two brunets, one bearded, one with a mustache, one blond with glasses, the other speaking German fluently going under the alias of von Jäger. The Gestapo would have known Group Boxer was in town. It wouldn't have taken them long to put two and two together. Counter-scorch would be compromised.

"What's your unit?" asked the major.

Chase felt like smiling. The major wanted to report him. How sweet, he thought. There was something touching about this Southerner, obviously a career officer, sticking up for noble principles. The Nazis can shoot prisoners, we can't. Noblesse oblige. It reminded Chase of the objections of a State Department official to the creation of the OSS: gentlemen don't read each other's mail. They

39

were sentiments with which a Yankee aristocrat like Chase was in complete agreement—in principle, for if there was one thing Chase's studies in political science at the University of Heidelberg taught him, it was that all moral rules and philosophical systems had to allow for exceptions if the society that spawned them was to survive.

"I can't tell you, I'm sorry. If I could, we wouldn't have had to do what we just did," he said, leaving it at that. He turned to the Kübelwagen. "Chris, Frank, climb on board."

"What about us?" the major started.

"Major, you have weapons, transportation and your lives. What more can you ask?" Romer and Kirilis climbed on board and Chase stamped his foot to signal D'Arcy. "Goodbye, Major," he said, saluting.

The Puma moved off, watched by the freed prisoners, agape. As they climbed the slope, Kirilis shouted over the noise of the engines, "People are funny. You save their lives and still they complain."

"Human nature, old man." Romer consoled him.

The conference between the Boxers and the partisans was held in the villa with all the solemnity of a boardroom meeting. On one side of the dining table sat Chase and Romer, on the other the partisan delegation. There were three men in it, Piero-Piero, a broad-shouldered bull of a man with hands like spades who had fought in the Spanish Civil War; Bluter, a gaunt, Moscow-trained political commissar whose skin had the pallor of one who had spent too many years in Fascist jails; and Dario, a short stocky factory foreman who was in charge of party membership. All three struck Chase as dour, suspicious, and humorless. Genuine Communist revolutionaries, Chase told himself. He opened the proceedings with a short speech:

"We represent the Allied High Command. I am instructed to pass on the following message from General Clark. The Allies will shortly launch their offensive for the north. General Clark is counting on the partisans to help him. The Allies have learned that the Germans intend to wreak maximum destruction as they leave, in accordance with Hitler's scorched earth policy. In this particular area, the Germans intend to blow up every industrial installation. Our mission is to help Italian partisans prevent the Germans from destroying La Spezia. The operation to save La Spezia is code-named Counter-scorch. It will entail the creation of small commando units, each responsible for a specific installation. At a signal from the Allied High Command, these groups will attack and overpower the guards, dismantle the demolition charges, and hold the installation until the arrival of the Allies. I am empowered to negotiate an agreement of cooperation between the Allied High Command and the La Spezia Committee of Liberation. Counter-scorch has the approval of the General Command of the Volunteers of Liberty," Chase concluded.

Piero-Piero leaned back in his chair. "An operation of this size will require a very large force. And it will have to be armed with modern weapons. Our armament is primitive."

"The Allies will supply you with modern weapons," replied Chase. "These could be parachuted in a day or two."

"Will the comrades who take part in this operation be paid?" Dario asked.

Chase nodded. "They will receive the same pay as Italian army soldiers fighting on the side of the Allies."

"What about the families of comrades killed in action? Will they be compensated?"

"Yes, on the same basis as Italian regular soldiers fighting with the Allies."

Both Piero-Piero and Dario looked at Bluter.

The other leaned forward with his arms on the table. "Who will be given credit for this operation, you or us?"

41

"The partisans. The operation will be described by Radio Fighting Italy as a partisan rising."

Bluter nodded, satisfied.

Piero-Piero glanced at Dario. The other nodded. Piero-Piero turned to Chase. "We are prepared to discuss co-operation."

The negotiations got underway. First the money. Chase proposed wages of five hundred lire a day, the partisans asked for one thousand. They settled on seven hundred and fifty lire, equivalent to $7.50 at the official rate of exchange down south. A cigarette ration was agreed upon: eighty cigarettes a week. Compensation for wounds and death was negotiated. Medical supplies. Uniforms. The partisans insisted on those because of the standing this would give the partisans in the community. Chase agreed to uniforms and berets, but refused to give in to their request for red stars on the berets. A food ration was established. Next, policing duties—and the first bone of contention cropped up.

"We understand there are plans to ship a thousand Carabinieri to La Spezia as soon as hostilities end," said Bluter.

"Law and order have to be maintained," Chase replied.

"The Carabinieri have besmirched the honor of Italy by cooperating with the enemy," said Bluter. "Their presence is unacceptable to the anti-Fascist forces."

"Who's going to police the town?" asked Chase.

"The partisans will police La Spezia."

And eliminate the anti-Communist opposition in the process, Chase said to himself. "Very well, I will communicate your objection to the Allied High Command." He turned to Romer, who was taking notes. "Unresolved."

They moved on to other matters. Reintegration of partisans in civilian life, disarmament, separation pay. When those had been agreed on, they turned to numbers. How many men would be required for the operation? The partisan proposed five thousand. Chase countered with one thousand and handed the partisans a list of Counter-scorch targets with the number of men that would be allotted to each. The list had been prepared after another meeting with Szendroy, who had given the Boxers the latest information on the number of soldiers guarding the demolition charges. The Boxers planned to assign fifty men to the hydroelectric power plant; three hundred men to the harbor installations; two hundred men to the oil refinery and petrochemical plants; and three hundred men to the industrial park, where there were about thirty factories.

"That leaves you a force of one hundred and fifty men, which we propose as a mobile reserve," said Chase.

"Ten men per factory," said Piero-Piero. "That is nothing."

"The factories are lightly guarded," replied Chase. "At any one time three men is the most there are. And most of the guards are not German but Ukranians and Poles, and other nationalities from German-occupied territories. As you must know yourselves, such guards are unreliable. Then, too, the factories in the industrial park are not that large. The large ones are in the oil refinery complex, and you will see that there the groups work out to thirty men each."

"We have information the Germans intend to reinforce the guards much beyond their present strength," Piero-Piero countered. "In some cases, the guards will be tripled."

"You must also realize, Capitano, that our soldiers are not regular army troops," said Dario. "They are brave, certainly, but they don't have the training of the regular army. Their lack of training has to be compensated by numbers." ·

"We cannot agree to take part in Counter-scorch with so few men," said Piero-Piero. He looked at Bluter as if inviting him to confirm this. But the other kept his eyes

43

on the pencil that he was slowly turning between his fingers.

"To undertake such a large operation with a thousand men is to commit suicide," said Dario. "For it to succeed we will need at least five thousand men."

"Very well," said Chase, "I will communicate your objections to the Allied High Command." He turned to Romer. "Unresolved."

"What kind of arms would you send us?" Bluter asked.

"Stens, ammunition and grenades."

"A thousand men armed with Stens and grenades," Bluter said with scorn. "You really want this operation carried out on the cheap."

"Commissario, you know yourself the factory guards are armed with old rifles."

"Yes, but those reinforcing them will be armed with Schmeissers and heavy machine guns and even cannon," said Piero-Piero. "Stens won't be much use against cannon. We will need machine guns, bazookas—and cannon."

"A few minutes earlier you told me your men were inexperienced," Chase reminded him. "How can they handle cannon?"

"We have a few cannonieri who deserted to us from a Fascist destroyer," said Piero-Piero. "They will teach the others. We partisans learn quickly."

Bluter looked up from his pencil. "We must have artillery."

"Very well, I will pass on your request," said Chase.

They discussed a few more points, then broke, with Chase promising to communicate the partisans' counter-proposals to the Allied High Command that very evening. He and Romer walked them to their Fiat. There were stiff goodbyes and the partisans drove off.

"Cannon, can you imagine," said Chase, watching them go. "Next they'll ask for tanks."

"What's their game?"

"They're using Counter-scorch as a bait to obtain arms so they can arm the factory workers for a Communist takeover." They turned to go inside. "It will be interesting to see how Russel reacts to their demands."

"What do you think Russel will answer?"

"I don't know. If we don't give them what they want, they might tell us to go to hell and La Spezia goes up. If we give them all they want, a Communist revolution might succeed and those factories out there will be nationalized. An interesting dilemma for Jim Russel."

"Hey you guys!" It was Kirilis calling them from the garage. "Come round to the back. We've got a surprise."

They walked to the back. At the umbrella table on the back terrace sat four women in nurse uniforms.

"I arrested them for trespassing," said Kirilis in French.

Three of the women laughed, understanding French. The fourth, a blackhaired woman with green eyes, questioned D'Arcy in Arabic. After D'Arcy had translated Kirilis' remark for her, he said to Chase and Romer, "This is Clara. She's from Libya." In an aside tone he added, "I have a feeling she will be Mrs. D'Arcy."

"Tanto piacere, Signorina," said Romer, taking her hand.

"Tanto piacere," said Chase, following suit.

"Parlate italiano?" exclaimed a vivacious redhead.

"Certo," replied Romer, going to shake her hand.

"This is Francesca," said Kirilis, placing his arm on the back of her chair in a gesture that indicated Francesca was bespoken.

Next came a baby-faced but well-endowed blonde. "Silvia."

Next, a tiny thing but with pep. "Rosanna." Romer sat down next to her.

Which left Chase with Silvia.

"Seems it is common practice for the nurses to cut across the villa property to get to the bus stop," said

45

Kirilis. "There's a gate in the wall and no lock. I told them they'll have to pay a fine."

"What's the fine?" asked Romer.

"Lessons in Italian. The first one is tonight. They are coming to dinner."

The sun was going down and church bells were tolling the Angelus as D'Arcy began preparing for the evening radio transmission. The first thing D'Arcy did was to attach suction cup hooks to the four walls of the library near the ceiling. Then he stepped down from the chair and went to a table where the radio lay, an SSTR-1 short-wave transmitter-receiver packed in a small suitcase. Attached to the inside of the lid were two coils of wire. He took the first coil, plugged one end into the radio, then proceeded to criss-cross the room from hook to hook in the shape of an *X*.

"I'll be glad when we get the new sets," he remarked, hanging up the last of the wire. "They need hardly any aerial."

"How long is this one?" asked Kirilis, standing watch by the window.

"Seventy feet." He went to get the other coil, again plugged one end into the set, then snaked it along the floor to a water pipe so as to have a grounding for his set. "Done," he announced, looking at his handiwork.

To an untrained eye, stringing aerials and earth wires was hardly handiwork, but to a professional radio operator like D'Arcy it was art. First there was the pattern of the aerial. Like an artist who goes through his blue or cubic period, D'Arcy was going through his cross period, having gone previously through triangular and rectangular periods. In the course of the last few missions he had strung aerials in the shape of eleven crosses: Egyptian, Swastika, Maltese, the cross of Lorraine, to mention a few. The *X* was his twelfth cross, the cross of St. Andrew.

46

The earth wire, too, was an artistic endeavor. It was always laid in the shape of undulating waves, the goal here being not variation as with the aerial, but perfection. In this case D'Arcy could be compared to a Japanese brush painter who will spend a lifetime painting the characters of the alphabet over and over, a Zen form of art to which D'Arcy was introduced by Romer. Before the war Romer had traveled in the Far East, exploring for the National Geographic Society.

"You're making progress," said Kirilis, eyes on the snaking wire. Once he used to make fun of D'Arcy, but after being exposed to snaking wires for over a year he was developing an affinity for this form of art. "I mean it, there's something to it. I don't know what it is, but I know it's there."

"It's the flow," said D'Arcy. He gave the wire a final glance and went on to other things. He unscrewed a bulb from a lamp in the ceiling and screwed the radio's power line into the socket. He plugged the morse key lead into the set and tested the current. Then he went to join Kirilis by the window. "Any sign of them?"

"They should be here any minute. Szendroy said they were leaving."

They stood in silence watching dusk settle over the town and the lights go on. Kirilis pulled out a pack of Popolare and lit one. "How's Paola?" he asked.

"I only stayed there a few minutes, long enough to pick up the radio," said D'Arcy. "She has a nice apartment. Full of antiques."

"Does she live alone?"

"I don't know. Why? Do you have designs on her?"

Kirilis laughed. "Not anymore, not since I met Francesca. Francesca is more my type. Paola has a lot going for her, but she's too serious. I like gay women." He took a drag. "Clara is all right, too."

"Yes, she looks as if she could be a tiger," said D'Arcy.

47

"It's going to be an interesting experience making love to a woman in Arabic. I've never done it."

"You mean in all your time in Egypt you never had a woman."

"Not an Arab woman. The only women I had dealings with were European: Greek, French, English, but never Arab."

"How come?"

"Arab women are very concerned with their virginity."

"Then what makes you think you'll make out with Clara?"

"Clara's not Arab. She's Italian. She was only born there."

There was the crunch of gravel and the Aprilia drove up the driveway. It came to a halt in front of the garage and Chase and Romer got out.

"Buona sera," said Chase, looking up.

"Buona sera," replied D'Arcy. He tapped his wrist-watch.

"Veniamo, veniamo," said Chase.

"Toss you for who stands guard by the gate," said Romer. He flipped a lira.

"Croce," said Chase.

"Croce it is," said Romer. He pocketed the coin. "If I see any D/Fs I'll whistle 'Giovinezza.'" A Fascist song.

Chase entered the house and climbed the stairs to the library. He handed D'Arcy several sheets of paper with columns of letters, the message in code. "I am afraid it's very long, but Szendroy wanted to include his recommendations."

"What's he recommending?" asked D'Arcy, taking the sheets to the table with the radio.

"That we should stick to our guns. He says that stuff about German reinforcement is pure fantasy."

D'Arcy sat down by the radio table. He turned on the set and put on the earphones, the left phone on the ear, the right one off to the side. He took off his watch and

48

placed it on the table facing him. "Paola was asking about you," he said.

"Was she now?" Chase replied noncommitally.

"I get the impression you're her first choice," said D'Arcy, exchanging glances with Kirilis. Ribbing Chase about his attractiveness to women was a favorite sport in the group.

"That's nice," Chase replied. He took a book off the shelf and flipped through it.

"You should have seen Paola this afternoon," D'Arcy went on. "Ten times better looking than yesterday."

"Considering that yesterday she was soaked to the skin, that's not surprising." He replaced the book and went to the window.

"We've ordered dinner for eight," said Kirilis.

"Good, I am starving."

"Frank, I think you should go now," said D'Arcy. "I told the hotel manager we'd come before seven. He speaks French. You don't mind standing in for Frank, do you, Nick? We have to pick up the booze."

"Go ahead," said Chase. He moved to the other side of the window so as to be able to see Romer better.

Below, the town's lights were coming on. What Chase would have given at that moment for the prospect of dinner followed by bed. He was dead tired. Four hours' sleep today, three the night before, four the night before that. After a while a man started feeling it. He wasn't eighteen anymore, but twenty-eight. He really wasn't feeling in a mood for a partouze, he decided, but that's what was in the air. Jeff, Chris, Frank, all gave the impression of stallions in heat. And the nurses weren't coming to the villa to pick flowers either. The speed with which they accepted the invitation, and the looks they gave them, confirmed this.

"Got it!" exclaimed D'Arcy behind him. Rome had answered his call sign. He put a hand to the left ear-

49

phone, a habitual pose of his, and began transmitting. The staccato sound of a morse key filled the library.

Chase watched Kirilis drive the Aprilia down the driveway as he went to collect the liquor. He hoped the nurses wouldn't drink too much. He couldn't stand drunken women, and Kirilis had a knack for getting them drunk. The professional seducer.

The telephone rang downstairs. Chase decided to let it ring. He didn't want to leave the window. A lot of things could happen in thirty seconds in their business. But the caller persisted and the ringing began to get on D'Arcy's nerves.

"Answer that phone!" he shouted, without pausing in the transmission. "It's driving me nuts."

Chase ran downstairs. "Pronto."

It was Szendroy. "Do you have any candles?" he asked. "My lights have gone out."

"Candles?" asked Chase. Then it hit him. He slammed down the receiver and shot upstairs. "Cut!" he shouted to D'Arcy. "Radio game."

"Car battery!" D'Arcy shouted back, continuing to work the key. To take the radio off the mains and plug it into a car battery was the standard countermove to a radio game.

"Can't. Frank took the car."

"Then play it!"

Chase started. Normally when no battery was available the operator broke the transmission there and then. Instead, D'Arcy had decided to play the enemy at his own game, hoping to outfox him. It was a dangerous ploy, but there was a certain logic to it. With Counter-scorch, every hour counted. And then there was a certain panache to pushing your luck as far as it would go. It was the sort of thing Chase did all the time in his field. Now D'Arcy was doing it in his. Chase went to the window. Szendroy's house was on the right side of the bay. Question was, would the enemy work horizontally or vertically? The answer came seconds later. The enemy was working horizontally, the gods were on the Boxers' side. A section of the port dimmed.

"Cut!" said Chase over his shoulder, bringing his arm down. The room fell silent.

The lights came on. "Go!" The morse key went into action.

"They will double-check!" D'Arcy shouted, his hand working the key, eyes following the columns of letters.

Once again the lights in that part of the port were extinguished.

"Cut!"

The lights came on. "Go!"

A moment later the telephone rang in the La Spezia Gestapo headquarters. It was from a Gestapo agent at the town's electricity board informing the station that the secret radio transmitter was in such-and-such area of the port (because when the electricity was cut there, the transmitter went off). Four D/F vehicles were immediately dispatched to the scene to narrow down the transmitter's location. The vans arrived on the scene and turned on their equipment only to discover that they had been had. By the time the electricity board resumed its power cuts D'Arcy was off the air. The report on the partisan conference had got through. Now there would be no secondary transmission to interrupt their party.

In peace men dream of adventure, in war they dream of good food and women. In this respect the Boxers were lucky: their war was accompanied by plenty of both, operating as they did far in the enemy's rear. In the rear, away from the front lines, there was no shortage of food provided you had the money. The black market was there for that purpose. And the Boxers had money, lots of money. One thing the OSS wasn't short of was gold. Its millionaires made sure of that. There were quite a few in the higher echelons of the OSS and they used their connections to keep the coffers full. While such people had no qualms about using the agency to keep friends in business, they did make sure the agency was suitably rewarded. Kramer Industries wasn't getting the services of the Boxers for free. Counter-scorch was a two-way street. So with no money problem, there was no food problem.

As for women, they too were available in large numbers. Alone and often lonely, the ranks of their menfolk reduced by death and prison camps, they were eager for male companionship. It was the Boxers' job to take advantage of this. World War II was total war in more than one respect, and women were involved in it as much as men. With their ability to pass unnoticed where men would attract attention, their talent for turning feminine charm to ruse, and their loyalty once they had committed their hearts, women were invaluable allies. More Boxer missions owed their success to women than to guns and explosives. The Boxers were well aware of this, which is why they always treated women with gallantry and consideration.

In keeping with this policy, considerable effort was being expended to make the soirée a night the four nurses would remember for years to come. A Boxer party was no spaghetti-and-meatballs snack followed by a tussle in the hay. A Boxer party had class. The man in charge of the evening preparations was D'Arcy, ably assisted by Kirilis. The two men represented the group's entertainment committee. D'Arcy headed it by virtue of his cooking ability; he was a first-rate cook. In addition he had two other qualities that made him ideal for the role: he was a fanatic for cleanliness and a stickler for etiquette. Kirilis was on the committee because of his experience with seducing women. He had made a study of what women liked and didn't like, what made them tick. After "blowing things up," women were his next interest.

"I think we should put out some lights, don't you?" he said. "Women don't feel very comfortable with a lot of light around."

"Wait," said D'Arcy, examining a wine glass against the light. "Nick," he called over his shoulder. "These glasses are filthy. They need to be washed again."

The leader of Group Boxer, freshly shaved and showered and dressed in a dark suit, appeared from the sitting room where he had been helping Romer. Without a word Chase collected the glasses and took them to the sink in the scullery. D'Arcy and Kirilis exchanged looks. Shafting Chase was another favorite team sport. The opportunity didn't arise too often. That's how old scores were paid back in Group Boxer. It was all done in the spirit of maintaining a healthy relationship rather than malice. Everyone had his turn at giving it and having to take it.

In the sitting room Romer continued selecting records in the order in which they were going to be played. Kirilis decreed they had to be selected in advance. He didn't want the postdinner mood broken by awkward silences with couples standing on the floor making polite conversation while someone searched for a suitable record. Mood was very important to women. Kirilis wanted the music continuous, the dancing nonstop. The evening had to flow, without any interruptions. Seduction, like everything else, was a question of planning in advance. With this in mind, Romer was arranging the stacks with fast numbers at the top and slow at the bottom. The dancing would begin with quicksteps and sambas and rumbas, and progressively slow down to tangos and slowfoxes and finally to smooch music.

"Did you put out fresh soap and towels in the bathroom?" asked D'Arcy, arranging flowers on the table. He brushed a speck off the white tablecloth.

"Yes, I did," said Kirilis, laying out the cutlery.

"What about the toilet bowl?"

53

"I cleaned it."

"Good."

The front door bell rang and Romer went to get it. Outside stood waiters carrying trays with platters. They unloaded them in the kitchen and went away. D'Arcy called the others in. First he told them what the seating arrangement was going to be at the table, then he explained the menu. That way they could speak knowledgeably of the food if the ladies asked. It was attention to such detail, from clean toilet bowls to knowing your sauces, which made the Boxer dinners the elegant soirées they were.

"We'll begin with trenette in pesto. Trenette are those noodles." D'Arcy pointed to the appropriate dish. "The sauce, pesto, is made from basil leaves with a little butter and garlic mixed with oil, pine seeds, and sharp cheese. It is a specialty of the region. With it we will serve a white wine, also of the region. The name is Cortese di Liguria. That's the stuff in the ice buckets. The main course is called vitello all'uccelletto, roast veal flavored with sage to give it a game flavor. With it comes . . ." The briefing continued.

At half past eight there was a knock on the back door of the villa. As if at a signal, lights dimmed and the record player rolled with dinner music. Nails were inspected for the last time, combs passed through hair. In keeping with his position as chief host, Chase went to open the door.

"Amigos! Caballeros!" A dazzling Francesca stood at the door. "We are here."

"Greetings Señoritas!" Chase ushered them with a deep bow. He watched them breeze in in their low-cut dresses, perfume swirling, faces made up; four women out to have a great time.

The night was on.

The air in the dimly lit sitting room was heavy with the scent of perfume and cigarette smoke. The only light came from a small red-shaded lamp placed out of sight behind the sofa. On the record player the table turned with Salomone's "Sono tre parole . . . Ti voglio bene," a slow, melancholy love song. The carpet was rolled from the floor. In the middle of the room two couples swayed in rhythm to the music: Chase and Silvia, and Romer and Rosanna. The others had left the room, D'Arcy and Clara to look at books in the library, Kirilis and Francesca for a starlit walk in the garden.

Out of the corner of his eye, Chase could see Romer's hand travel up and down Rosanna's spine without too much reaction from Rosanna. Either she wasn't interested, or she was playing hard to get, thought Chase. Silvia on the other hand was much more encouraging, her flaxen hair pressed into his cheek, her stomach close to his. In fact had Chase wanted to he could have left the room some time ago. But he wasn't sure he really wanted to. Paola's visit had left him with a mental block.

Paola had arrived at the villa shortly after the dancing entered its slowfox stage, asking for the radio. Szendroy wanted her to send a message to Rome on the 0200 cast. The Boxers, of course, had asked Paola inside while D'Arcy went to fetch the transmitter. It only took him a minute, but it was one of the longest minutes the Boxers had ever lived through as they watched Paola's reaction to the soirée: her cold manner towards the other women as if they were usurpers, her eyes taking in the use her flowers were being put to, ignoring the Boxers' attempts at small conversation.

They felt like heels. Yesterday this woman had been the apple of their eye. She had braved rain and thunderbolts to reach them. She had even risked her life. Thanks to her they did not have to spend a wet night on the beach. Thanks to her there was food for them when they arrived. And what did they do as soon as they were on dry land and rested? Did they send her flowers? Did they throw a dinner in her honor? No, they forgot about her and devoted their energy and charms to four pickups instead.

The man who felt the biggest heel was naturally enough Chase. It was in his direction that Paola's parting look of reproach was addressed. For Paola to be slighted by men like D'Arcy or Kirilis or even Romer was bearable. None of them was Paola's kind of man. But Chase was, just as Paola was his kind of woman. Both knew this. There had been an empathy between them from the start. To have Chase shower her with looks of admiration and gratitude one moment, and to see him with a new woman twenty-four hours later was, for Paola, a slap in the face.

"What's wrong?" asked Silvia sweetly.

The question brought Chase back to the present. Silvia had a point. For an Argentinian he was unusually slow. In Europe, Argentinians had a reputation for being men of action. The question also made him realize he would have to sleep with her or at least make a pass. To have one woman on his conscience was bad enough. To have two was too much.

"I have a bit of a headache," he answered.

"If you like I will cure it for you," said Silvia. "I know how."

"You can cure headaches?"

"My brother is a chiropractor. He taught me. It's done by twisting the neck."

"Twisting the neck?" Chase exclaimed.

"It won't hurt. Don't worry."

"If you're going to twist my neck, we'd better go up-stairs," he said after considering the proposition. "We don't want to spoil their romance," he added with a nod in Romer's and Rosanna's direction. "I scream easily."

They went upstairs to his bedroom. There was a

56

straight-back chair and she told him to sit on it. She went to stand behind him and took hold of his head, one hand under the chin, the other on the back of his neck. The hold reminded him of something they had learned during close combat training at the Farm in Virginia.

"Are you sure it won't hurt?" he asked.

"You won't feel a thing," she replied. "But you must relax." With that she began turning his head gently, first to the left, then to the right. "Relax more."

"I'm trying, I'm trying."

"Breathe in and hold your breath."

He took a deep breath. Crack! He felt his neck snap out of joint, except that it didn't. It was merely the sensation.

"Did it hurt?" asked Silvia.

"No."

"Is your headache gone?"

"I think so. I don't feel it anymore."

"Then it's gone."

He got up and took her face in his hands. "Thank you." As his mouth closed over hers, her tongue plowed into his mouth and she pressed herself close to him. Right away he knew she was a greenhorn. It wasn't a French kiss, it was an open-mouthed fish kiss.

"Turn off the lights," she murmured.

He turned the light off and took her by the hand to the bed. They lay down and began kissing. More fish kisses. After a while his hand went to her breasts.

"No," she said, pushing it away.

Too early? thought Chase. They kissed some more, then his hand went to her thighs.

"No," said Silvia, crossing her legs.

It occurred to Chase that perhaps Silvia did not want to make love. Perhaps she was one of those women who were content with necking. She was after all rather young and innocent looking. Fair enough, he didn't mind. But it was getting hot, so he decided to take off his jacket.

57

As he moved away from her, however, she grabbed him and pulled him to her.

What now? thought Chase. Perhaps Silvia was shy about her breasts and thighs, he told himself. Perhaps he should try another approach. Chase's hand went to the zipper at the back of Silvia's dress.

"No," said Silvia, pushing the arm away.

To hell with it, thought Chase. If it's no, it's no. He moved away to rise. Silvia grabbed him by his shoulders and pulled him to her violently.

After that there was only one thing left for Chase to do, do a Romer. With his women Romer used the Neanderthal Man approach. The phrase was his own. He would pick them up chair and all, carry them with the chair to the bedroom, throw them on the bed, and start biting their breasts, through the dress if necessary. Chase's approach would be a half Romer, minus the chair, which was just as well because few men could do that without panting. Romer could, being strong as an ox.

Chase took hold of Silvia's wrists, pressed them down on the bed, and sank his teeth into her left breast. Silvia gave a half cry half moan and began struggling, fighting him off. Chase tightened the wrist hold and bit the other breast.

"No, no, no," Silvia panted. "Let me go!" she cried while pressing her leg between his thighs.

It was high school stuff and several times Chase was on the verge of throwing in the towel. Fighting flaying arms and legs was all right at eighteen when you were so hard up you'd put up with anything to get a bit of sex. But at twenty-eight you didn't have to. You could get plenty of the same at a much more leisurely and enjoyable pace. Nevertheless he did put up with it, mainly because he was a gentleman, and a gentleman, he knew, tries to please a woman, which in bed means doing it the way she wants it. Silvia had always dreamed of being taken the way gauchos did it in the Argentinian pampas. A novel she had read on the subject had left a vivid impression on her. Silvia wanted to be ravished. So that's what Chase did, he ravished her. In the process he made himself a friend and assured himself of the success of Counter-scorch, for it was thanks to Silvia that the mission was saved from disaster. But this he had no way of knowing at that moment, and in any case he wasn't even thinking of Counter-scorch. He was thinking of Paola. Now that he had done his duty to this woman, he felt the urge to do at least the same for the other. He glanced at his watch.

"What time is it?" asked Silvia, catching the gesture.

"Nearly twelve-thirty."

"I must go soon. I am on duty at six." A sigh of pleasure escaped her lips and she nestled up to him. "I would like us to stay so all night."

"All good things come to an end," said Chase paternally. In her presence he felt old enough to be her father. It was partly her face, partly her attitude of making love and also those fish kisses of hers. He could see himself addressing her as "my child." Saying to her, "My child, when you kiss, you don't open your mouth as far as it will go." For the moment, however, he said, "If you have to go, let's go now." He gave her a paternal kiss. "It's so nice we might both fall asleep."

They dressed and went downstairs. The sitting room was deserted, the record head grating at the end of a disc. It was obvious that Romer had had his hands full when he left the room, otherwise he would have turned off the record player. Perhaps Rosanna too wanted to be taken by force.

In the hall he took Silvia's coat from the cupboard and helped her to put it on. Then they went out the back door into the garden. It was a warm, starry night and the air was heavy with the scent of flowers.

"Isn't it beautiful?" exclaimed Silvia, looking up at the mass of stars.

They walked towards the gate in the wall, Chase with his arm around her. "Do you always start work so early?" he asked.

"I was supposed to have worked tonight, I mean right now, but I changed with another girl whose shift starts at six so I could come to your party."

"I hope it was worth it," said Chase.

"It was," she replied, putting her arm round his waist. She looked up, pressing close to him and smiled. Her gaucho!

They reached the gate and turned to face each other. "Would you like us to see each other again?" he asked.

She nodded eagerly. She took his hand and fondled it. "My last name is Moscatelli. When you want to see me, leave a note at the front desk and I will come round. Don't phone, they don't like it."

"Good night." He bent down and got another fish kiss.

Then she broke off and went through the gate. From the other side she blew him a kiss. "Ciao."

Back in the villa, he paused at the foot of the stairs, hand on the railing, head bent in thought. Bed or Paola? The body urged bed, the heart Paola. The heart won out. Chase hurried upstairs to D'Arcy's room and knocked gently. He got no answer so he knocked louder.

"Yes?" He heard D'Arcy answer from inside.

"It's me, Nick. I want to speak to you."

"Wait. I'm coming." A sleepy woman's voice asked a question, D'Arcy answered in Arabic, there was the sound of bare feet and D'Arcy came out, closing the door behind him. "What time is it?" he said, blinking and tightening his bathrobe.

"A little after one," said Chase. "Where does Paola live?"

D'Arcy looked at him incredulously. "You're not going to visit her at this hour, are you?"

"She has a transmission at 0200. Someone should keep

D/F watch for her. The Germans might start another radio game."

"Where's Silvia?" asked D'Arcy.

"She's gone home."

"Ah!" D'Arcy nodded knowingly. Chase had failed to score with Silvia. Now he was going to try Paola under the pretext of D/F watching.

"Silvia has to work early," added Chase, reading D'Arcy's thoughts. "What's Paola's address?"

"Sixty-four Via Strozi. Apartment eight. On the top floor. And if you really intend going there, I suggest you call her on the phone first. Tell her you're coming so she doesn't go into a panic when you knock on her door."

"What's her telephone number?"

"Four, zero, nine, nine, one," D'Arcy quoted from memory. They were trained to keep addresses in their heads. On top of which he had a photographic memory.

"How do I get there?"

D'Arcy gave him directions. "And I'd take a weapon. A radio guard without one isn't worth much. That's if you really are going to guard her."

Chase ignored the doubting Thomas jibe. "Thanks."

He went to his room and took a quick shower. He didn't want to spoil his good deed by smelling of another woman. When he was dressed he took the Schmeisser and his ammunition vest and went downstairs to the phone. He dialed Paola's apartment.

"Si?" she answered guardedly.

"Nico here. I'm coming over." He put the receiver down.

From the cupboard in the hall he collected his trench-coat, which the hotel had washed that afternoon, and went to the car. He hid the weapon and ammunition in the compartment and drove to town. He had twenty minutes in which to get to Paola's.

The Aprilia sped through the night, the wind rushing through the open windows. He was driving along the Corso George Washington, a wide boulevard with a cobblestone roadway lined by tall date palms. To get to Paola's he had to cross town and this was the fastest route. He was the only traveler on the road. The streets were empty and the intersections deserted. The only sign of life came from the all-night bars outside which military vehicles were parked. Chase glanced at his watch. He was going to make it. But his luck changed. As he was approaching the intersection of Via Mazzini, the town's main north-south street, he was waved down by a German military policeman. A roadblock.

"Buona sera," said Chase, holding out the curfew pass Szendroy had given him earlier in the day.

The Feldwebel in charge of the patrol waved it away. "Convoglio," he explained in German-accented Italian. He motioned Chase to cut the engine. No point in wasting gas.

Diable! Chase swore to himself. He toyed with the idea of turning around and trying another street, but realized that they would have similar roadblocks. They probably had them the length of the convoy route. He switched off the engine and glanced at his watch again. If the convoy came quickly he might just make it.

The convoy came almost immediately, but it took ages to pass. There was truck after truck, many of them towing artillery pieces. Reinforcements for the Gothic Line to the south. By the time the last truck passed, it was well after two.

"Avanti," said Feldwebel, motioning Chase to resume his journey.

Chase drove on, asking himself whether he shouldn't turn around. It was too late to be of any use as a D/F watcher. The transmission would be over by the time he got to Paola's apartment. On the other hand he did say he was coming so she might be waiting for him. He decided to go there anyway. He would explain he was held up by the convoy.

In Piazza Verdi, two blocks from Strozi, he saw two D/F vans outside an all-night bar. The crews were on the sidewalk, mugs of beer in hand, laughing and talking loudly. They gave the impression they were celebrating. A celebration! The word ballooned in Chase's head. Goosepimples broke out on his skin and a strange feeling materialized in his stomach. A premonition.

As he turned into Strozi, a narrow one-way street, all his fears materialized. Parked on the curb on the left side were two large black Mercedes-Benz convertibles. The license plates were German and the cars were unattended, a sure sign they belonged to the Gestapo. The Gestapo never worried about their cars being stolen; only a madman would try that. Slowly Chase drove by, trying to read the numbers over the doorways of the apartment houses. He couldn't make out the others, but he was able to read the one beside the cars because of a streetlamp, sixty-four.

Chase's hair stood on end. Paola in the hands of the Gestapo. Counter-scorch compromised. The Germans would get it out of her, no matter how brave she was, he was sure of that. It was one thing to stand up to the Gestapo when they weren't sure of their case, when they might have made a mistake, it was another when they caught you redhanded. Psychologically the difference was enormous. They probably wouldn't even bother with torture, Chase thought. A slap or two perhaps, but mainly it would be interrogation, perhaps with a hint that her parents might be arrested. Basically they would do it the way lawyers did it in court, tying the witness in knots. Chase cursed himself for not telling Paola about the radio game when she came to pick up the transmitter.

At the next intersection he turned right and stopped the car to get the Schmeisser and collect his thoughts.

At all cost he must prevent Paola from being taken to the station for the interrogation. He had to strike now, before they even drove away. The question was where to jump them? In the apartment, on the stairway, or as they were coming out onto the street? As he weighed the possibilities, it occurred to him that perhaps he shouldn't be thinking of jumping *them,* perhaps he should be thinking of jumping *her.* It was the sort of unpalatable thought that he normally left to D'Arcy to voice. Trouble was they weren't in this together. He was alone and so he had to do his own dirty thinking. One part of him, Chase the gentleman, the man with a heart, hated himself for even thinking it, but the other part, the professional OSSer, continued the process. To take on two carloads of Gestapo was risky and not very productive. To aim for Paola and run was far less risky and more productive. With Paola dead, the Gestapo would have no way of knowing about Counterscorch. Nevertheless even the professional OSSer realized he had a moral obligation in this case. It was conceivable that had he not phoned her, she would have run when she heard knocking, taken to the roof, or used some secret staircase. Instead, expecting him, she opened the door.

As was his habit, he did not wait to decide this way or that way. Experience had taught him that the solution lay in action. By initiating action he created a situation where he was forced to do things by instinct. And instinct was amoral. What you did by instinct you never regretted. So he put the Schmeisser on his lap, put the car in gear, and drove around the block to reenter Storzi. As he did so, he saw a sight that sent adrenaline pumping into his system, clearing his mind of thought. Paola was being led out the doorway of the apartment house by two men in leather coats and fedoras. Two other men, similarly dressed, were already in the front. He saw the taillights come on. For some reason he was sure the other Gestapo men would not be coming, a perfectly logical supposition because the apartment of a radio operator was usually

64

searched, or more precisely ripped apart, and that took several hours and several people to do. Now instinct took over.

He accelerated slightly and drew alongside the Mercedes-Benz as the last Gestapo took his seat in the back. "Servus!" he called out, using a well-known Austrian greeting. He pointed the Schmeisser through the window and pulled the trigger. There was a string of hisses and the men in the front seat exploded with bits of brain and blood. Bullets thudded into wood and metal and the windshield shattered. Paola and the men in the back ducked. Chase burst out of the car, ran to the Mercedes, and jabbed the nearest man with the silencer-cylinder at the end of the barrel. He pulled the trigger, and the man cried in pain and went limp.

A window opened on the upper floor. "What's going on?" a man in a leather coat shouted, leaning out. In answer a stream of lead rose with another string of hisses towards the window. The man withdrew screaming, hands clasping his bloody face, the window shattered and fell to the pavement. On another floor a light went on, then went off again as some curious tenant thought better of it.

"Nick, look out!"

Chase threw himself sideways as the Gestapo man crouching on the floor of the Mercedes pushed Paola aside and fired his pistol. Chase rolled, seeking the protection of the car as other bullets thudded into the roadway from pistols fired upstairs. The Schmeisser hissed and more glass fell as bullets sprayed the window. The Mercedes swayed as Paola fought the Gestapo man. Chase went down behind the bonnet and changed magazines from the vest under the trenchcoat. He duckwalked to the back of the car, fired another burst at the window, then sprang to his feet. He jabbed the Gestapo man and fired. The man gave a cry and collapsed.

65

"Run for our car," said Chase. "You drive. I'll cover you."

Paola jumped over the side and ran while Chase kept the Gestapo upstairs away from the window with short bursts. In the distance he could hear the pim-pam, pim-pam of a police car alerted by the pistol shots. Or maybe the Gestapo had used the telephone to call them in? As he fired, Chase backed to the Aprilia. Paola was turning over the engine but it wouldn't start.

"Press the accelerator pedal right down," said Chase.

A bullet whizzed past his ear, embedding in the roadway. He let off another burst, did a lightning magazine change, and followed with more bursts. The Aprilia came to life just as a police car turned the corner, tires screaming, a block behind them. Chase stepped onto the running board.

"Let's go!" he shouted.

The Aprilia shot forward, Chase spraying the window a final time. He pointed the Schmeisser at the police car, but nearly fell off. So he threw it inside and followed through the window, feet first. In the OSS they were trained to do that.

"Head out of town," he instructed Paola. "That's a radio car." In town, with a radio car on their tail calling in other cars, they'd never get away.

Paola took the car through several side streets, then came out onto a wide boulevard and accelerated. The Aprilia streaked past deserted streets and intersections, the roar of its exhaust filling the night. The police Fiat, its blue light flashing, pim-pammed behind them. Paola threw Chase a look as if she was rediscovering him.

"What was that for?" he asked, intrigued.

A playful, slightly seductive expression crossed Paola's face. "You must be my guardian angel. This is the second time you have saved me."

Chase smiled. Her guardian angel, he liked that. He took the Schmeisser and changed magazines, then un-

66

screwed the silencer. They might be in for some prolonged shooting and prolonged automatic fire burned out silencers. He put the cylinder in the pocket of the trenchcoat and settled back to enjoy the ride. He liked the way Paola drove, the fast yet relaxed manner in which she changed gears, the way she held the steering wheel, arms outstretched like a racing driver. It was a sexy sight.

"Where did you learn to drive?"

"Cino taught me. Before the war he raced cars. Then he crashed and Papa forbade him to race anymore."

"And where did you and Cino learn English? You speak it like natives."

"Our first nanny was English."

They sped towards the coastal road. Paola threw him another look. "Where are we going, Genoa?"

The devil-may-care way in which she asked this gave the impression she wasn't very concerned by their predicament. Nor was he for that matter, which was curious because they were in a real pickle. On the other hand, he said to himself, perhaps it wasn't curious. It was Paola's presence that caused his lack of concern, he decided; she was one of those women who by a process as mysterious as womanhood itself gave a man confidence. A woman you could go stealing horses with, he said to himself. It was a German expression.

"We'd never make Genoa," he replied. "As soon as that car knows which direction we're going, they will radio ahead for a roadblock." He paused to think, then asked, "How far is the nearest forest?"

"The forest of Tremoli is about ten kilometers from here. It's on the road to Pisa. That's going the opposite way."

"Let's head for there."

They reached the coastal road and turned south. On their right lay the sea bobbing with lights from fishing vessels, on their left sand dunes and factories. After a kilometer or two, the road left the coast and turned in-

67

land, snaking into the hills. Behind them the Fiat disappeared and reappeared from round bends, the driver maintaining a constant distance between them, a good two hundred meters at least. The crew was playing it safe. Rather than catch up with the Aprilia and risk a shootout, they were passing the buck to the people who would be manning the roadblock.

At the thought of the roadblock Chase experienced uneasiness. Something told him to get off the road now, not to wait for the forest. A genuine premonition or his imagination playing tricks? he asked himself. Like everyone Chase had had his share of premonitions that turned out to be duds. What was certain, though, he told himself, was that by driving on like this they were leaving everything to chance, abandoning themselves to fate, instead of taking the initiative. He began looking about him, eyes piercing the darkened countryside. The road took them through farmland interspersed with woods, the famous chestnut woods of Liguria whose nuts were used to make flour for Liguria's chestnut bread. Some of the woods they passed through were quite large and had trails coming up to the road. Trouble was, he only saw them at the last moment. To get into them would mean stopping, backing, turning, a long process. They were bound to be seen by the car behind them. Then an idea occurred to him.

"Paola, do you know how to turn a car quickly?"

"You mean like they do in American gangster films?"

"No, not quite. That's called turning on a centesimo. I am talking about a three-point turn. First you bring the car to a quick stop, then—"

"I know what a three-point turn is. Cino taught me."

"Could you do it?"

"What, now?"

"Not yet. When I tell you. First I might tell you to accelerate. Then, when I tell you 'stop,' I want you to hit the brakes, quickly turn, and accelerate. You think you can do that?"

"I think so."

"I am going to the back," said Chase, climbing over the seat. "When the police car passes I will fire. You may be hit by spent shells. They burn a little but that can't be helped. After we pass the Fiat I will tell you to turn off the road onto a trail into a wood, so be prepared to do a quick turn. Capito?"

"Si, Generale."

"For your information I am only a captain," said Chase from the back.

"Maybe for the others. For me you're a generale."

"Thank you for the promotion." What a lark! he thought. Flirting in the midst of a car chase.

Chase wound down the window in the back and peered through the gloom, looking for trails. The road snaked through a large wood, up, down, left, right. Several trails went by but he ignored them. They had no landmark, he wouldn't be able to recognize them on the way back. Then they flashed by a trail with a broken tree at the junction, freshly broken probably from the previous night's storm. Ahead was another bend. Behind, the police car was several bends behind.

"Accelerate!"

The Aprilia picked up speed, round the bend, down, up, round another bend to a flat stretch. This was the place to do it, he said to himself.

"Stop!"

The Aprilia screeched and he was thrown sideways as Paola performed her own version of a turn on a dime, sending the car skidding to a halt almost facing the way they had come, almost in a ditch too, but not quite, and wonders of wonders, the engine hadn't stalled. Instead it was already working on reverse. Chase found himself on the floor and they were off, Paola changing gears like a racing car driver.

69

Round the bend, down, up. The inside of the Aprilia lit up from the headlamps of the oncoming Fiat. A deafening hammering filled the Aprilia's interior, spent cartridges flew everywhere, flames from the Schmeisser probing the night. The Fiat flashed by, the Aprilia's interior reverted to darkness, a pair of taillights disappeared behind a bend.

Did he get it? He didn't know, the two cars passed each other so quickly. And before he could recall his memory, his mind was occupied by other things. Over Paola's shoulder he was scanning the left side of the road for the entrance to the trail. Then he saw the tree, its gash shining white in the light of the headlamps.

"Turn left by that broken tree," he said. "Immediately after."

Without bothering to slow down, Paola drove the Aprilia into the trail. There followed a mad two hundred yards with the car bouncing and slithering over bumps, ruts, and leftover pools of water, Chase holding on for dear life. They turned a bend.

"Stop and lights out."

The car slid to a halt, Paola cut the engine and doused the lights. A silence settled over the Aprilia. In the distance an owl hooted. The wood was still. Then they heard it, the pim-pam, pim-pam of the approaching police car. It shot past the wood towards La Spezia.

Paola turned and kneeled on the front seat facing him, arms resting on the back supporting her chin. "Well, Generale?"

In answer Chase leaned forward and kissed her. "Come to your guardian angel," he said, drawing her to him over the seat.

There followed one of those sublime moments of intimacy bred of shared danger, the fusion of two hearts united by adventure.

The noise in the wood was like an aviary. It was morning, bright and sunny.

"Good morning, angel," said Paola, leaning over the front seat. They had slept in the car, she in the back, he in the front. "What are we doing for excitement today?"

He propped the back of his head with his hand and smiled. "More of the same, I hope."

They held each other's smiling eyes, conscious of their new relationship, recalling the night's pleasures. It had all been so wonderfully natural, as if they had known each other all their lives.

Then he remembered Counter-scorch. He sat up briskly. "How good are you at walking?"

"Are we going to walk back?"

"We can't use the car. The police will be looking for it." He surveyed the trail. "Any idea where that could lead to?"

"The beach, probably. We are near the sea. Can't you smell it?"

Chase sniffed the air through the open window. "I smell chestnuts."

From her handbag Paola took a comb, adjusted the rearview mirror, and with long strokes began combing her hair. "I don't think it would be wise for us to walk back."

"Why?"

"We will arouse suspicion. Only peasants walk, and we don't look like peasants. We would be safer to go by sea. We could rent a boat. There's bound to be a fishing village in the vicinity."

"That's a thought," said Chase. He paused to consider it. "Okay, let's try that."

At Paola's suggestion, Chase took off his jacket and tie to look more informal. He made a bundle of it with his Schmeisser and ammunition vest, wrapped in the trenchcoat. Then they set off down the trail, holding hands. On the way he asked her about the Gestapo raid. They hadn't talked about that yet. Paola told him the Gestapo had arrived a few minutes after she had ended the transmission, knocking gently on the door. Thinking it was him, she opened it right away. They couldn't have caught her in a more compromising position. The radio was still on the dining room table, as Rome had asked her to stand by for a transmission by them an hour later.

"They made no attempt at playback?" asked Chase.

"No, I didn't tell them I was waiting for a transmission. I suppose they thought I had finished for the night."

The Gestapo told her they had been working to pinpoint her for several days, had narrowed the search to her street, had rented an apartment nearby staffed by agents with portable D/F equipment. Her latest transmission enabled them to establish that the signal came from No. 64, but she had gone off the air by the time they entered the courtyard so they didn't know which apartment to go to. They decided to search the whole house, starting with the top apartment, which turned out to be hers.

"Did they ask who you were working for?"

"Yes, that was the first thing their leader asked me. I told him I wouldn't say. He said we would talk of that more at the station. They were very correct."

"They would have been less correct in the station," said Chase. "Was there anything in your apartment to link you to Szendroy?"

"Nothing. Nothing to connect me with Henrik or Cino. When Cino and I went to work for Henrik we burned each other's photos and letters. Henrik told us to."

"What about record of expenses, or anything like that?"

"What expenses?"

"Expenses that you present to Szendroy for reimbursement."

"I don't present any expenses."

"Then how does he know how much to pay you?"

"Pay me? Henrik doesn't pay me. I am not doing this for money."

"Don't you even get expenses? Who paid for the gas you used to collect us the other day?"

"Cino and I did. I told you, we are not doing this for money. Is that so hard to understand?"

"No, it's not hard," said Chase, dropping the subject. But he made a mental note to raise the matter with Szendroy. The whole thing smelt of a combinazione: agent hires patriotic subagents to work for him, omitting to mention Control sends him their wages anyway.

They left the wood and entered grassland, the trail having shrunk to a footpath. The footpath led them to cliffs overlooking the sea where it branched north and south. They walked north and after a while saw a cove with a fishing village. They went down to it. By the village well women were washing clothes.

"Buon giorno," the women chorused.

"Buon giorno," Chase and Paola replied.

"Che bella ragazza," said an old woman.

"E vero, è vero," replied Chase gaily. With a smiling glance at Paola, he added, "E bellissima."

Paola squeezed his hand. To the old woman she called out, "Tanto gentile."

They continued to the beach, where men were sitting on stools, repairing fishing nets. In contrast to the women, there was no warmth from this lot. They watched the couple approach with indifference.

"Good morning," said Chase cheerfully. "Would you gentlemen know where we could rent a boat for the day?"

A momentary silence descended as the gathering considered this request. Then began a round of looks with which men who know each other well communicate. To Chase the conversation was as easy to read as a book.

Well, brothers, here is an opportunity to make some easy money. Who's interested?

73

Tarquino, what about you? This could get you out of debt.

Out of debt and into jail, no thanks. You can be sure there's something illegal about this pair.

What about you, Massimo? Illegality has never stopped you from picking up an extra few thousand here and there.

A young man in a top hat broke the silence. "Where would you be going?"

"La Spezia," said Chase.

"How many?"

"Just the two of us."

The man inserted a toothpick in his mouth and picked his teeth pensively. "Five thousand lire . . . in advance."

"Two thousand," Chase countered. He didn't want to give them the impression he was loaded.

"Four," said Top Hat.

"Three," said Chase.

"E fatto," the other replied. "When would you want to go?"

"Now."

The man nodded pensively. "That's my boat," he said, pointing to a felucca tied to the wharf. "I will meet you there." He rose and walked quickly to the village.

They walked to the boat. "That man gives me the shivers," said Paola. "Have you noticed his eyes? They are cruel."

"I don't like his eyes any more than you do," said Chase, "but we've got to get back to La Spezia and he's willing to take us."

They reached the wharf and sat down on some piles. The smell of fish was everywhere and seagulls circled overhead. Chase counted out three thousand lire. He didn't want to pull out his bulging wallet in front of Top Hat. They waited, gazing out to sea.

"You know, Nick," Paola said wistfully, "I wish we didn't have to go back. I wish that car chase had lasted forever."

74

"I know what you mean," said Chase sympathetically. Then he turned to her and smiled. "There are bound to be others."

The wharf shook as Top Hat came, accompanied by two pals. One was a skinny individual with a bathing cap on his head, the other stocky with a mass of wild hair. All three were in their early twenties.

"Have you got the money?" asked Top Hat.

Chase handed him the fare and they went on board. The trio went into the steering cabin while Chase and Paola sat on a bench in the prow. The engine came to life and they headed for the sea. The felucca was a grimy, smelly boat with an unusually powerful engine, a combination that usually denoted a contraband vessel. A fishing boat didn't need so much power. It was a beautiful day, the sky blue, the breeze cool, the water choppy, and the sun not too hot at that hour. Paola leaned back against the side and closed her eyes, soaking up the sun. But Chase kept his eyes open. The three characters in the booth kept glancing at them in a curious way, as if they were trying to decide something.

Chase suspected they did not take him for a native, despite his fluent Italian. In this respect Italy was difficult terrain for a secret agent, in some ways even more difficult than Germany. The Italians, he had observed, were interested in their fellow man to an extent greater than any other people in Europe. Also, Italians had a highly developed sense of detail for such things as dress and human behavior, from the way one walked to what you did with your hands when you argued. They seemed to notice many more things. For instance, ingenious aliases and disguises, to which escaped prisoners of war reverted and which would fool German officials, were noticed by the simplest Italian, one reason why so many POWs who escaped from Italians were immediately picked up. In his case his personality alone could give him away. A man with his air, his definite movements, and his confident look might pass for an SS officer, but hardly an Italian, at least not an Italian of that period, a tortured soul alternating between timidity and bravura. That was one reason why their cover was Argentinian.

"Nice day," said Top Hat, coming up to him.

"Very nice," replied Chase.

Top Hat picked his teeth, eyes on the sea. "Are you from far?" he asked, switching his attention to Chase.

"Tuscany," replied Chase. That would account for his blond hair. It would also keep him incognito as far as the authorities were concerned. If ever this man sang to the police about an Argentinian who materialized out of the woods . . .

"Your friend also from Tuscany?"

"Campania," said Paola without opening her eyes.

"Are you refugees?"

"Sort of," said Chase. "What about you, where are you from?"

"Rome." The accompanying look said, If you're from Tuscany I am from Rome. Top Hat resumed picking his teeth, looking at his feet. "My friends and me have been talking. We think we should renegotiate our agreement. We're losing money on this trip. I should have charged you more, *much* more."

Chase nodded attentively, but said nothing.

"My friends and me think this trip will cost us at least five thousand. Gasoline is expensive. So are port fees. They charge port fees in La Spezia. The minute you tie a line to the mooring, you pay." He paused to pick some more. "For this agreement to be fair, you should pay ten thousand."

"I'm sorry, I don't have that kind of money," said Chase.

Top Hat's eyes traveled to Paola's pearls, then to her gold watch, then to Chase's watch. "We would be agreeable to payment in kind."

Chase nodded slowly, his mind clicking fast. To keep

the conversation going served no purpose. It would be wishful thinking on his part. Top Hat would never back down. If anything his demands would grow. After Paola's jewelry it would be his wallet. And after that . . . into the sea. "Tell you what," said Chase. "Bring me a screwdriver." He tapped his bundle. "I've got a box here with some interesting coins. Perhaps we can reach an agreement. The box is locked." Holding the other's eyes, he added in a new tone, "The owner didn't have time to give me the key . . . if you understand what I mean."

Top Hat nodded. "I think I do. Let's see the box."

"First bring the screwdriver. And bring your friends too. I want all three of you on this together." Chase's tone hardened on the principle that people believe in nastiness more than in pleasantness. "No more of this talk of my friends think this and my friends think that. This time we make an agreement that is final."

"Bene," said Top Hat. "I'll get the screwdriver." He walked off.

Chase got off the bench and went onto deck on his knees. With his back to the steering cabin he proceeded to undo the bundle.

"What are you going to do?" murmured Paola, her eyes closed.

"Teach them a lesson," Chase replied. "Be ready to lie on your stomach. But first tell me when they come out of the booth."

Paola opened her eyes and began looking around as if getting her bearings. They were sailing parallel to the shore, several hundred meters from it. A lone seagull followed them. Its call could be heard above the noise of the engines.

Chase armed his weapon under the cover of the coat. He inserted a magazine, then gently cocked the Schmeisser. One hand on the grip, the other holding the coat ready to whip it back, he adopted a pose as if he were inspecting something, the box for instance.

"They're coming," said Paola.

Chase pulled back the trenchcoat and swiveled, weapon in hand. But the others had caught sight of it before he came to face them. He saw a black object hurtle towards him and threw himself sideways. The screwdriver swished by, imbedding itself with a thud in the deck behind him. He rolled to his knees only to throw himself again, this time to avoid a wrench. A burst of gunfire rent the air as Chase, now on his knees again, fired to stop Wild Hair's charge. The other buckled, hands clutching his chest, blood gushing from his mouth.

The others ran, Top Hat into the cabin, Bathing Cap further back. Chase fired again, this time at Bathing Cap, but missed. Then a pistol fired through the opening of the steering cabin. The bullet sang past Chase, missing his face by a fraction. He felt the heat. He dropped to his knee behind some crates and fired a long burst at the opening. Bullets tore at the wood, sending shavings flying. Out of the corner of his eye, he could see Paola stretched out on deck, hands over her head. He half rose, sending bursts into the opening, while walking sideways to the bundle. He changed magazines, fired a short burst, and charged the cabin. Top Hat shot out the side of the cabin, pistol in hand. Before he could fire, Chase mowed him down. Top Hat crumbled, wriggling like a fish, then fell still.

"Look out!" shouted Paola.

Chase ducked as a knife swished past him. He turned to reply but couldn't see his attacker.

"He's hiding behind the booth!" Paola shouted.

"Esci, alto le mani," Chase called out, telling Bathing Cap to come out, hands up.

In answer there was a crash of something overturning and the splash of a man diving overboard. Bathing Cap had chosen flight.

"Paola, go to the steering wheel and turn the boat!" Chase shouted. "We're going after him."

Paola ran to the booth while Chase checked the bodies. Both men were dead. He emptied Top Hat's pockets and found what he wanted, the boat's ownership papers and the driving license. He would need that in case they were stopped. He looked into Top Hat's wallet and retrieved his three thousand lire. Then he dragged the bodies to the side and pushed them overboard.

Paola turned the felucca around and the boat plowed through the choppy water after Bathing Cap. Chase went to the trenchcoat and screwed on a silencer. He didn't want to draw any more attention to the boat with gunfire. At this distance it could be easily heard from the beach. He walked to the bow, put the Schmeisser selector on single action, and waited for the distance to shorten. Ahead, Bathing Cap was breaststroking frantically, glancing behind him every few strokes. Chase aimed and fired twice. Bathing Cap flayed the water, which began turning red. Chase fired again. Bathing Cap fell still, turned on his stomach, and sank out of sight. Chase went to the booth, slinging the Schmeisser over his shoulder.

"Steer for La Spezia," he said, entering.

Paola turned the boat around again. "Take over for me, Nick," she said. "I am going downstairs. There may be some fresh water. I must wash."

Chase took over the wheel. The felucca rose up and down, plowing its way through the waves towards La Spezia. A tune entered his head and he began humming. For some reason, unknown to him, he felt unusually gay. The humming turned to singing, a rousing German soldier's song.

"Oh, take us from this country where the Duce can't keep peace,

"Where the partisans make war on us, a war they never cease,

"They lurk for us in every street, and every single night

79

"They blow our trains to smithereens with sticks of dynamite.

"Here in this cursed country, for weeks we have to wait

"For letters from our dear ones, their news long out of date.

"Here in this hated country, north, south, and east and west,

"We carry out our orders, we fight and do our best,

" 'The devil take this country,' the German soldiers cry.

" 'Oh, Führer, send us home again, don't leave us here to die.' "

"What's that song?" asked Paola, returning to the steering cabin.

"The Song of the Wehrmacht in Italy," replied Chase.

"You have a nice voice. But I didn't know you spoke German. Where did you learn it?"

"I went to university in Germany. My father was ambassador there for a while." He saw her give him another of her rediscovery looks. "What was that for?"

"You know, if I didn't know you, I could easily mistake you for a German. An SS officer, for example."

"Really?" he said, pretending this was the first time he had heard someone say that. He had heard it dozens of times.

"I think it must be those steel-blue eyes of yours."

He smiled and kissed her on the neck. "That's only because you heard me sing in German. Wait till you hear my Communist repertoire." He put his arm round her waist, the other hand holding the wheel, and began singing the Communist partisans' song.

"Avanti il popolo, alla riscossa,

"Bandiera Rossa, Bandiera Rossa . . ."

The felucca plowed through the waves for La Spezia.

The wind whistled through the grass and clothes flapped in the breeze. In silence the partisans awaited the coming of the planes, their upturned faces watching the southern horizon. There were several hundred of them standing on the slopes of hills around a valley where the planes would parachute the supplies. They wore civilian and military clothes or combinations: some had caps and berets, others were bareheaded, but all had the red neck scarf that in Italy was the badge of the Communists. For armament they had an array of weapons as varied as their clothes. A few were armed with the Variara, a machine pistol made in a secret partisan factory in the Apennines. The ones who had them were mostly officers. The troops had World War I rifles, some had only a pistol, some had nothing more than a grenade stuck behind their belt.

A young man with a Variara came up to Chase. He wore a hat with a plume, the headgear of the Bersaglieri, a famous Italian army unit. His name was Nino and he was Piero-Piero's right hand. He saluted Chase with a clenched fist. "Everything is ready, Capitano."

"Are the guards posted?" asked Chase.

"All are in place," replied Nino.

"Pass the word to the men to wait until all the planes have left before they begin collecting the crates," said Chase. "I don't want anybody killed by a falling container."

"I will do that, Capitano."

"And please tell Comandante Piero-Piero not to worry if the planes are not on schedule. They are often late."

"I will do that, Capitano." Nino gave another clenched fist salute, clicking his heels, and went off.

"Where did that salute originate?" asked Chase.

"In the Spanish Civil War," said D'Arcy.

They stood halfway down a slope from which they had a good view of the entire drop zone. Chase didn't want to

81

miss the container with the orange parachute, the one that would contain the money. There had been cases where after a drop all the containers were accounted for except the one with the money. In his hand Chase held a whistle, which he would blow when the B-25s appeared on the horizon to signal Romer and Kirilis to light the fires. At each end of the drop zone were piles of branches with rags soaked in oil, smoke signals defining the DZ for the planes. Ever since an incident in Albania, the top and tail bonfires were always manned by a Boxer. In Albania, as the planes arrived, the local partisans discovered no one had any matches. Not seeing the signal, the planes flew back without making the drop.

Chase glanced at his watch, then at the sky. The sun was going down. "Did Rome say how many planes were coming?"

"No, but they said we'll get all we asked for."

"How were they able to communicate with Szendroy?" asked Chase. "He only had one SSTR and the Gestapo have that."

"He doesn't need an SSTR to pick up Rome," said D'Arcy. "He can pick them up on a simple receiver. All the agents have them now: small, pocket size, shortwave receivers."

"Velivoli!"

The shout was picked up by others. Chase and D'Arcy scanned the sky for the B-25s. Instead they saw a solitary dot. Automatically they glanced about for cover in case the plane turned out to be enemy. Stories of people being shot up by enemy planes while waiting for a drop were legend. But there was no cover. The hill was bare except for scrub.

"Let's hope it's one of ours," said Chase.

A moment later D'Arcy identified it. With his photographic memory he knew all the silhouettes. "A Mosquito." Allied.

The light bomber headed straight for them. It flew over

the valley and went into a circling pattern, flying low. D'Arcy pulled out a torch.

"Who are you?" he flashed in morse.

The Mosquito flashed back, "Identify yourself first."

"Boxer," replied D'Arcy.

"Svenson," said the Mosquito. The OSS chief in Rome. "Dropping a Joan-Eleanor."

The plane broke out of its pattern, flew out, then flew back along the length of the valley. As it neared where the Boxers were standing, a container detached itself from a wing and a black and yellow parachute sprouted.

"Take over," said Chase, handing D'Arcy the whistle. He called to some partisans nearby and led them to retrieve the container.

They dragged it back up the hill and Chase opened it. The thing turned out to be not a Joan-Eleanor, but the British version of it, the S-phone, not that it mattered for it did the same job. With D'Arcy helping him, Chase strapped the battery belt round his waist, then harnessed himself into the braces, attached to which was the actual phone apparatus. That consisted of a rectangular box with a T-shaped antenna sticking out. Chase turned so that the antenna faced the Mosquito, now circling far out over another range so as not to attract the enemy's attention to the valley. He put on the earphones and turned the frequency knob to receive. Right away he picked up Svenson's call sign. He turned the knob to send, put the rubber mouthpiece over his mouth firmly so as to shut out outside noise, and gave his call signal. The conversation began.

"How are you? Over," said Svenson.

"Very well thank you. How are you? Over."

"I'm fine."

In the OSS it was considered cool to exchange pleasantries at the beginning of a ground-to-air conversation. There were those who did this even when under fire. Nonchalance was cultivated.

"Have the partisans signed?" asked Svenson.

"The signing is for tomorrow," said Chase. "There was no time to do it today. They want to organize a ceremony."

"How are they taking it?"

"They're not very happy. They say we're treating them like gun fodder, that with only a thousand men and no heavy weapons they'll be exposed. But they say they'll sign. Under protest."

"Under protest my foot. They're getting a bargain. Food, clothes, medicine, money, weapons. And all they have to do for that is hold up a few old men with rifles. Ninety percent of Counter-scorch is a simple inside job. Have you given them a list of targets?"

"That's all arranged."

"How much notice will you need?"

"They say four hours. Any indication when the Allied offensive is likely to start?"

"Very soon. Did you tell the partisans we agree not to send the Carabinieri?"

"Yes, I did. They are pleased. But Szendroy isn't. He says the Communists will organize a bloodbath. They'll wipe out the Christian Democrats and the Socialists."

"Tell Szendroy he has nothing to worry about. A unit of Special Force will supervise the partisans' police duties. Italian-Americans. They'll make sure there's no bloodbath. But keep this to yourself. We don't have to tell the partisans that now."

"Okay."

"So the signing is for tomorrow. Good. On no account are you to agree to any changes. Certainly not to any more arms."

A whistle blew as D'Arcy caught sight of the B-25s. Moments later flames licked the bonfires and black smoke from the oil rags rose skyward.

"We have information that two out of every three weapons we send the Communists in the north are immediately buried for use later on," Svenson continued. "Our

84

man in Milan says all partisan zones have received orders to this effect. You know what that means, don't you? They're gearing up for a coup d'etat. Trieste reports Russian officers are crossing into Italy from Yugoslavia as advisers. Yesterday near Turin there was a pitched battle between monarchist partisans and the Reds. Things are heating up. If we don't watch out . . ."

The rest of the sentence was lost in the roar of the B-25s. The sky filled with parachutes. Chase's eyes scanned the sky for an orange parachute. It wasn't there. Diable! he swore to himself. They forgot it. Now there would be more complications. The partisans would suspect him of trying to diddle them out of their money. He reverted his attention to Svenson. The Rome chief was talking about the situation in Greece where a Communist-led revolution had broken out to overthrow the monarchy. The British, whose royal family was related to the Greek King, were pouring in troops to crush it. The Greek revolution was an embarrassment to the OSS as it was the OSS, whose Athens chief was an antimonarchist Greek-American, that had armed the Communists in the first place. They had armed them over the objections of their ally, Britain, who warned them this would happen.

"We can't afford a repeat of the Greek fiasco," Svenson said.

"I understand," said Chase. "But Joe, where is the money? I don't see an orange parachute."

"Sorry, I forgot to tell you. I have it here. Thought it would be safer if we dive-bombed it to you. I also have two radio sets for Jeff. The nylons are with them. We'll drop the radios first, then the money."

"What's this about nylons?" said Chase to D'Arcy.

"Frank asked for them," said D'Arcy. "I tagged the request onto your message last night." He smiled sheepishly. "That's why we had to play the radio game—to get Frank's request through. It was at the end of the message."

85

Chase shook his head in disbelief. The frivolity with which they sometimes approached their work was amazing. A radio game for some nylons. Incredible! On the other hand, he said to himself, perhaps that was to be expected. You can get used to anything, even danger, like that Okie he met in a bar in New York. At first, said the Okie, cars petrified him. Then he got used to them. And now he was jaywalking like everyone else. So it was with the OSS. In the beginning one saw danger everywhere. Every policeman was suspecting you. You hardly dared to step out into the street. Then, bit by bit, you got used to it. Radio transmissions that used to be a hair-raising adventure, or so it seemed at the time, became first a routine, then a bore. Now to get a kick out of life, to feel a spark of danger, people resorted to playing radio games—for nylons. Such distractions had become part of their life, just like shopping by radio had become routine. But then why not? Everyone, he reflected, had his own way of milking the agency, Russel to protect an investment, Kirilis to pursue his amours. In France D'Arcy had finished a radio message with a request for condoms. They arrived with the next drop.

The sky roared as the Mosquito flew over. A container with a red and white parachute sailed to the ground. Then the Mosquito came for its second pass. This time it flew much lower. As it neared Chase a sack free-fell to the ground, narrowly missing a mule loaded with crates. The pilot dipped his wings and the Mosquito headed south while in his earphones Chase heard Svenson say, "There's enough dough there to last you a week. If you need more let me know. Don't blow the gold. No point in wasting that if they're willing to accept lire. Be talking to you on the cast tonight. So long."

"Have a good trip back," said Chase, switching off the phone.

They walked down the slope. The floor of the valley was a beehive of activity. Crates and containers were being loaded on the back of men and mules. On some slopes columns of men and animals were already winding their way out of the valley.

"Have you noticed something?" said Kirilis, joining them. "Their mules don't bray. You know why? Their vocal chords are cut. Isn't that clever?"

They commandeered a mule and driver, loaded it with their goods, and went to see Piero-Piero. The partisan commander stood on a slope surrounded by his staff, looking very revolutionary in a black leather jacket and a Spanish Civil War beret with a red star. A Variara hung over his shoulder.

"Are you leaving?"

"Yes," said Chase.

"Who was in that Mosquito?"

"Our commanding officer. He came to make sure everything was going well."

Piero-Piero threw Chase a look of doubt, then turned to Nino. "Drive the Capitani to La Spezia." He gave the Boxers a farewell nod. "A domani."

The road, a stony dirt track, wound through desolate hills of rock and scrub. The headlamps of the van, another Bianchi, picked out butterflies and the odd animal—a wild cat, a fox. Once they even thought they saw a wolf. Here and there they passed woods. Occasionally they caught sight of lights from some lonely habitation. It was the sort of countryside you drove through without stopping, thought Chase, for to stop was to get depressed, depressed by a land whose rocky soil was good for hardly anything, depressed by the houses smelling of urine and droppings, the animals occupying the ground floor, the humans above them, depressed by the changeless, stubborn, backward people. In silence, listening to the sound of the engine, Chase brooded. But there was more to his brooding than simply the countryside. There was

87

Paola. No sooner did they get back to La Spezia that morning than Szendroy announced Paola had to leave town. The Gestapo were circulating her picture and had posted a reward of 50,000 lire. It was too dangerous for Paola to remain in La Spezia. She was known and she could easily be betrayed. Chase recalled Paola's pleading eyes when Szendroy announced his wife would drive her to Genoa, eyes that seemed to say: do not send me away, let me share the rest of this adventure with you. Have I not given a good account of myself so far? Why are you afraid to take risks now? Did you not say that together we could conquer continents? But Szendroy was adamant. When Chase said he needed Paola for Counter-scorch, Szendroy hit the roof, accusing Chase of callousness, of being willing to risk Paola's life for the sake of ambition. It was an unjust accusation, but it did open Chase's eyes to how wrong he had been about Szendroy. In their heated exchange it came out that far from exploiting Paola and Cino, Szendroy was playing godfather to them. Every month he sent a sum of money representing their wages and expenses to their parents in Genoa. The parents put the money into a special account and the money would be given to Cino and Paola on the day of their marriages as a wedding present from the OSS. Szendroy was doing this without Cino or Paola's knowledge. Both had refused to accept wages or expenses on grounds that a true patriot did not fight for money. When he heard that, Chase realized that he was in the presence not of Paola's boss, but something more, almost family. The family didn't want Paola to end up a corpse in a Gestapo station and the family was right. He had to agree to Paola's going. Then came the heart-wrenching moment when he held her in his arms for the last time in Szendroy's sitting room, the two of them left alone by Szendroy.

"Will I ever see you again?" Paola had asked, tears in her eyes.

"Probably not," he replied. Out of principle he never made promises to women. Nor did he tell them he loved them simply to make them feel better. To him that was cheap.

Paola lay her head sideways against his chest. "We are like two ships in the night."

"Yes," he said, caressing her hair.

"Don't you think that is sad?"

"No."

"I do."

"Paola, one day when you're a mother of four with a balding husband you will look back on these few days and you'll be glad you lived them. In life one regrets what one didn't do, not what one did."

Paola looked up at him, smiling through her tears. "I didn't know you were also a philosopher, Angel."

Chase smiled back. "Not a very profound one, I am afraid."

"And you," she asked, "when you are a balding father of four, will you think of me?"

"One day I will have sons and they will ask me what I did in the War. That's when I will tell them about my mission is Italy, how a beautiful woman appeared out of a storm to guide me to safety, how bad men tried to take her away from me on two occasions, how I fought eight men single-handed to save her, how the beautiful woman and I raced in a car in the night, because the beautiful woman was a very good driver. I will tell them all that and more. And I will always thank Providence for having brought us together, even though it was only for two days."

Lovingly Paola drew him to her until their lips met. Then suddenly she was on fire, kissing him passionately, her heart thumping wildly, her body on fire. In despair she cried, "Hold me, my Guardian Angel, hold me! I am not a philosopher and it breaks my heart that our love is destined to be but a memory."

• • •

The Bianchi screeched to a halt, the engine stalling. Before them a barrier of logs blocked the road. "Ma, che?" exclaimed Nino without finishing the sentence.

Chase's eyes registered the scene. To the right, a ten-foot cliff, to the left, the ground sloping gently. "Everybody out and down the slope," he hissed, dousing the headlamps and withdrawing the key from the ignition.

They piled out of the van, leaving the doors open so as not to make noise, and ran down, Chase carrying the sack with the money, D'Arcy and Romer the radio suitcases. They stopped by some boulders, unslung their weapons, and crouched.

From the hill atop the cliff a voice shouted in Italian with an English accent. "Friends, do not be afraid. We are British soldiers. We have to requisition your vehicle. But we will not harm you."

The others glanced at Chase. He put his finger to his lips.

"Why don't you say you are Americans?" said Nino.

Chase silenced him with a wave of his hand. Nevertheless the suggestion did make him think twice. If they did not identify themselves, the British would try to take the van and the Boxers would have to shoot at them. The absence of an ignition key wouldn't stop the British. They were probably from the Special Air Service, units of which were to be parachuted behind the lines in conjunction with the offensive, and those people knew how to start vehicles without keys. On the other hand, if the Boxers did identify themselves they would be breaking explicit orders, not to let anybody know they were OSS. The exception was the partisan high command. For obvious reasons they had to know. But no one else, above all not Allied commandos met by chance, muscle boys very good at killing silently, but very bad at remaining silent during an interrogation. When captured, and in Italy they were always being given away, they sang like canaries. Then it

90

occurred to him he could identify his group as Americans and leave it at that.

"This is Captain Jones of the United States Army!" Chase shouted in English. "We regret we cannot let you have our truck. We are also on a special mission."

The voice on the hill replied in English, "You speak very good English whoever you are. Unfortunately for you we know that the only Allied unit operating in this sector is ours. But a good try all the same. Please return to your vehicle and turn on the engine and the lights. Before we leave you will be given a receipt for the van."

A burst of gunfire broke the night's stillness and a flare shot into the sky. As it exploded they caught sight of a line of men in berets descending the hill abreast, probably to take the van. They saw the SAS soldiers throw themselves to the ground as tracers flew from Schmeissers and a Spandau, which opened up from the right side of the hill.

"The krauts to our rescue," exclaimed Kirilis. "Who'll ever believe this?"

"They must have been following them," said D'Arcy.

The Boxers watched in fascination as the two sides fought each other, green tracers going one way, red ones the other. Then grenades came into play. Flash! Bang! Flash! Bang! The Boxers could feel the blast of the explosions on their faces. All round them hills reverberated with the noise of the battle.

"Hey, this is like a war movie," exclaimed Kirilis.

"Che facciamo ora?" said Nino nervously.

"Aspetta," said Chase.

Another flare burst in the sky. By its light Chase saw two SAS men climb the hill from the road near the logs. That's what he had been waiting for. He had purposely held back running for the Bianchi for fear there might be SAS soldiers by the barrier. And so there had been. But now they left to join their comrades locked in battle. The coast was clear.

91

"Okay," said Chase, "here's what we do. First we remove the logs. Then into the van and we take off. Jeff drives." He handed him the keys. "Jeff takes both radios and goes directly to the van. After we clear the road, everyone in the back and I go in front. Let's go."

They raced for the road, D'Arcy bent double under the weight of the two suitcases. Above them the hill flashed with explosions and there was the constant chatter of Stens and Schmeissers, interspersed by the hammer of the Spandau. In less than half a minute they had the logs out of the way. They ran into the van, leaving the doors open. Closing them would make a noise.

"May Allah be praised," intoned D'Arcy, turning the ignition key. Stalled engines, he knew, had a habit of taking time to start. The Bianchi burst to life on the first turn. As the van shot forward D'Arcy switched on the headlamps. They tore down the road, the Boxers shutting the doors. The flashing hill receded until it disappeared from view behind a corner.

Eleven kilometers from La Spezia they ran into a road-block. They were on the coastal road now.

"Guardia," said Nino from the back as the headlamps picked out the black uniforms.

"Brake or gas?" said D'Arcy.

Chase took in the scene: the striped barrier, a dozen soldiers, a van, and an amphibious Fiat with a mounted Breda machine gun. The stance of the soldiers was relaxed.

"Gun it!"

The Bianchi shot forward, the barrier loomed towards them, the soldiers by the road reached for their guns. The van crashed through the barrier to the sound of breaking wood and twisting metal. Glass tinkled, and one of the headlamps went out. Behind them muzzles flashed briefly before they turned a bend.

"Anyone see a radio antenna?" asked Chase. None had. "We're okay then."

"No, we're not," said D'Arcy, eyes on the sideview mirror. Behind them a flare rose skyward, exploding in a shower of red.

At that a wood on the right lit up with a pair of head-lamps. The headlamps proceeded to move towards the road. D'Arcy pressed the gas pedal as far as it would go. The Bianchi shot past before the headlamps reached the road.

"What was that?" said Kirilis.

"Another amphibian," said Chase.

"Very clever. Just like a speed trap."

"They must have been sleeping," said Chase. The amphibian's reaction to the flare was slow.

"Well they're wide awake now," said D'Arcy, eyes on the side rear mirror again. "They're gaining on us, too."

The Bianchi raced along the winding road, D'Arcy negotiating the bends with tires screaming. But after every bend the headlamps following them grew larger.

"They're going to catch up with us!" shouted D'Arcy.

"Chris, open the back door and start shooting," said Chase.

Air rushed in as Romer opened the rear doors. There was the sound of bolts being cocked. The amphibian appeared from behind a corner.

"Aim for the headlamps!" Chase shouted.

The inside of the Bianchi reverberated with the hammer of machine pistols and bouncing cartridges. The air became permeated with the smell of sulphur. On the amphibian a headlamp went out.

"Bravo!" shouted Nino.

The next moment he was a mass of blood as the Breda atop the pursuing vehicle opened fire. Tracer bullets thudded into the Bianchi, ripping wood and metal. Three bullet holes sprouted in the windshield.

93

"Momma," moaned Nino, toppling forward, hands clutching his chest.

"Nino's hit!" shouted Kirilis as the firing ceased, a bend blocking the amphibian's line of fire.

The Bianchi reached the botom of a hill, bumped over a narrow bridge, and shot up a steep hill. Something scraped along the floor. Before Romer or Kirilis had time to react, Nino was gone, followed by his machine pistol.

"Nino's fallen out!" shouted Kirilis.

Behind them tires screeched, there was the sound of a crash, and an explosion lit up the countryside.

"They've blown up!" shouted Kirilis.

D'Arcy brought the Bianchi to a halt. "Guide me!" he shouted, reversing the van.

With Romer guiding him, D'Arcy backed the van round the last bend. The place was lit red. The amphibian Fiat lay on its side burning. Nearby lay Nino, dead. Romer and Kirilis dragged the body into the Bianchi and they took off.

"How the hell did that happen?" said Kirilis.

"Nino most likely," said D'Arcy. "At that speed, the smallest obstacle can throw a vehicle out of control."

"Poor Nino," said Romer. "Bravo one moment, morto the next."

"Shit!" Kirilis exclaimed. "I'm bleeding."

"Maybe you've been hit," said D'Arcy over his shoulder.

"Shit!" Kirilis swore again. "I have been hit."

"Where?" said Chase, turning in his seat.

"My arm. And I'm bleeding like a pig. Goddamnit, my brand new suit ruined."

"Where's your flashlight?" Chase asked D'Arcy.

"Under the seat with the radios."

Chase retrieved it, climbed over the seat, and inspected the wound. "You're lucky. Went clear through. I'll make you a tourniquet. That will stop the bleeding. Where are your nylons?" Nylons made excellent tourniquets.

"No way," said Kirilis. "Use my shirt. Those nylons are for the girls."

Chase took off his own shirt, ripped it, and made a tourniquet on Kirilis' arm. "There," he said, tying the final knot. "That'll do until we get back."

The back door bell rang and Romer went to open it. Outside stood Silvia and Francesca, the latter holding a first aid kit. Both were in white uniforms.

"I received your message," said Francesca. "Who is ill?"

"Franco," said Romer. He led the women into the dining room where the Boxers were finishing dinner.

"Bonsior chèrie," said Kirilis, rising. He had washed himself and put on a new shirt.

"Povero bambino," said Francesca, giving him a kiss. "What's the matter, caro?"

"Let us go to the sitting room," said Kirilis.

"Buona sera," said Silvia, giving Chase a conspiratorial smile.

"Buona sera," said Chase, kissing Silvia on the cheek.

Kirilis led the nurses into the sitting room. The other Boxers remained in the dining room. Kirilis took off his shirt. "I got hurt here," he said, pointing to the temporary dressing Chase had put on.

Francesca set down her first aid kit on a table.

"What is it?" she asked.

"A wound," replied Kirilis.

"A wound? What sort of a wound?" Francesca undid the dressing. "Franco!" she exclaimed. "This is a bullet wound. What happened?"

In the dining room the Boxers exchanged glances.

"Some bandits shot at us while we were driving," explained Kirilis.

"Bandits? Where? Sit down. Silvia, bring a bucket so

I can throw this somewhere. Where did they shoot at you?"

"In the hills."

"In the hills? What were you doing in the hills?"

"We went for a drive."

"At this hour?"

"We had a flat tire."

In the scullery Chase was going through the cupboards looking for a bucket. He found one and handed it to Silvia.

"I dreamt about you all night," she whispered, pressing close to him. She lowered her eyes coyly. "What we did last night," she said, moving her hand up and down his chest, "can we do it again? But not tonight. I have to work tonight. Tomorrow?"

Chase smiled. "Anytime you like." He followed her into the sitting room.

Francesca was dabbing Kirilis' wound with disinfectant. "Who cleaned this wound for you?" she asked.

"Nico did," replied Kirilis.

Francesca paused to look at Chase. "Where did you learn to clean wounds?"

"In the boy scouts," Chase replied.

Francesca threw him a dubious look. She glanced at Kirilis, then back to Chase. "Who are you?"

"What do you mean?" said Chase, taken aback.

"You're not Argentinian economists. I know it."

"Why do you say that?"

"Well for one, economists don't go into the hills. There's nothing for them to do there. And I don't believe you are Argentinians either. You know, I haven't heard you speak Spanish once to each other. You either speak French or Italian. Who are you?"

Chase and Kirilis exchanged glances. Both knew what the other was thinking. There's a point where it is safer to let the other person in on a secret. Otherwise they start discussing their curiosity with others.

"If we tell you," said Chase, "will you promise to keep it a secret?"

"Scout's honor," said Francesca, raising two fingers. "I was in the girl guides."

"Can we tell Rosanna and Clara?" asked Silvia.

"Yes, but no one else. Promise?"

"I promise," said Silvia.

"We are Americans," Chase announced.

"Americans!" Silvia shrieked with joy.

"Didn't I tell you?" said Francesca. "I told you they weren't Argentinians. I knew it."

"Americans!" Silvia repeated. "I have always wanted to meet Americans. Do you know Chicago? My mother's brother lives there."

"Didn't I tell you they were more like Americans than Argentinians?" said Francesca.

"What made you think we might be Americans?" asked Chase, intrigued.

"Because you don't treat a woman like Latin men. You are, you have . . . come si dice . . . you are more reserved."

"You find me reserved?" exclaimed Kirilis. He prided himself on being a hot blooded Greek.

"Even you, caro," said Francesca. "But it's nice. I like it. It's different. It makes a woman feel safe."

"Safe?" Before a true Greek a woman trembled, whether from fear or desire. But a Greek who made a woman feel safe? Jesus, what a comedown!

"Are you soldiers?" asked Silvia.

"Yes," said Chase, "we are with the Special Force. We attack German convoys."

"Ma!" exclaimed Silvia. "Is that what you were doing, is that why Franco is wounded?"

"Yes. Franco was very brave today," said Chase. "Actually, now that you know we are Americans you can call us by our real names. He's Frank and I am Nick."

"Nick," Silvia repeated. "Nick. Mi piace."

"Mio bravo Frank," said Francesca, giving Kirilis a kiss. "Mio bravo Americano. But I prefer Franco. E più romantico."

Kirilis smiled, basking in adulation. "Say chèrie," he said, as she ended bandaging his arm, "why don't you come back when you finish work and we'll have another party. Clara and Rosanna are coming later."

"But we must work tonight, caro," said Francesca.

"All night?"

"All night. Silvia and I are bed sitting a general." She added teasingly, "A very handsome general, too."

"Who's the general?" asked Chase.

"General von Rota. He is the comandante of the German soldiers in La Spezia. Very handsome."

"Abandoned for a very handsome general," said Kirilis, putting on a dejected face. He looked at Chase. "How do you like that? Me, a bravo Americano being outdone by a crucco." Crucco meant kraut.

"Caro," said Francesca, caressing his face, "I am not abandoning you. Your Francesca will be here like a sparrow first thing in the morning to awaken you. Anyway, tonight you need rest."

"What's he like, this von Rota?" asked Chase. "Apart from being handsome."

"A perfect gentleman," said Francesca. "Isn't he, Silvia?"

"Very nice. Today he sent Francesca and me a bouquet of roses each."

"The partisans say he is a war criminal," said Francesca, "but I would rather have him as a patient any day than one of those partisans. They are dirty and rude."

"And cocky," added Silvia.

"Is the general really a war criminal?" asked Chase.

"That's what the partisans say," said Francesca. "They hate him because he had a hundred partisans executed for throwing a grenade into a German social club. I say he was right to do it. Throwing a grenade into a social club,

98

can you imagine? What animals! Well, we have to go, or our supervisor will be docking our pay." Francesca gave Kirilis a tug on the ear. "And you to bed." She collected her first aid kit.

They walked them to the door and kissed them good-night. "Ciao." Then they closed the door and went to the dining room.

"You handled that very well," said D'Arcy.

"What time are Clara and Rosanna coming?" asked Kirilis.

"Eleven o'clock," replied Romer.

Kirilis emptied his wine glass. "I guess it's an early night for me." He turned to Chase. "What about you?"

Chase replied, "I guess it's an early night for me too. For once."

The signing ceremony was for nine o'clock in the morning. By eight, all four were downstairs dressed in dark suits, putting the final touches on the preparations. In the sitting room stood a long table that they had found in the garage and was to serve as the signing table. For lack of green baize they covered it with a bedsheet that easily passed for a tablecloth. The table was decorated with red-white-green flags for Italy and a bowl of red roses for Communism. They had borrowed the flags from the hotel next door. On one side of the table were chairs for the principal personages of the partisan delegation, on the other side two for Chase and Romer. Everyone else would stand. Piero-Piero said a dozen people would attend. There was even to be a reporter from *Il Partigiano*, the partisan newspaper. Before each chair was laid out a four-page manuscript containing the clauses of the co-operation agreement. They had been brought the previous night by Szendroy. Following the signing, everyone would move to the dining room where the table was laid out with platters of snacks, also brought from the hotel that morning: sandwiches of all sorts, boiled eggs, caviar, salmon, and cakes. To drink there were many varieties of wine, and vodka. The last was D'Arcy's idea. As many of the partisans had done their political training in Moscow, D'Arcy thought it would be a nice touch to remind them of their happy times in Russia. It was unlikely any of them had tasted vodka since, because in Italy it was hardly obtainable and when obtainable very expensive. To get his, D'Arcy paid the hotel barman in gold. Finally there was coffee, real coffee, with milk and sugar.

"Did you clean the bathroom?" asked D'Arcy, while arranging glasses in the dining room.

"The toilet bowl is spotless, the sink is dry, and the faucets are shining," replied Kirilis.

In D'Arcy's scale of values a bathroom was the most important part of the house. It was there that the character of the people who lived in the house showed itself in its true light. As D'Arcy's mother used to say, if you want to know what a person is really like, don't look at the sitting room, look at the bathroom. In keeping with this, Boxer bathrooms were the cleanest on the street, be the villa in Helsinki or Leopoldville. The sink was wiped dry and sparkled, the faucets shone like equipment in a fire station, and the toilet bowl was fit for a bath.

"Hey, Nick," Kirilis called out to the sitting room. "After the signing why don't we sing for them 'Bandiera Rossa.' I'm sure they would be impressed to see that we know it. Or we could do it in the dining room. You propose a toast to the partisans and then we all sing."

"That's a thought," said Chase, counting the money he was going to give the partisans. Since Slovakia he always counted such monies three times. There he had counted it twice as was his habit and still made a mistake. The local partisans didn't say anything but reported the matter to their government in London, which got in touch with the London office of the OSS, which radioed Chase in Czechoslovakia requesting an explanation. Not only had the incident been embarrassing to the agency, it had been embarrassing to Chase. One of his weak points was arithmetic. Even as a stockbroker, his profession before the war, he had a hard time working out profit and losses for clients because of his lack of talent for mathematical calculations.

"If we have a toast to the partisans," said Romer, licking caviar from a finger, "we should follow it up with a toast to Nino's memory. But for Nino none of this would be taking place. We'd all be dead. That Breda would have made mincemeat out of us. I can still see that thing belching fire at us."

"I think you're right," said Kirilis. "We definitely should have a toast to Nino."

"Might be an idea to contribute some money to the funeral as well," said Romer. "We could make a presentation to his brother."

"Nino's brother is coming for the signing?" asked Kirilis.

"That's what he said last night when he came to pick up Nino's body," said Romer. "He told me Piero-Piero has appointed him to Nino's post."

"Nick," said Romer, going into the sitting room. He repeated his suggestion. "What do you think?"

"Excellent idea," said Chase. "How much do you think we should give?"

"Ten, fifteen thousand."

"Let's make it fifteen." Chase counted the money and put it in one of the envelopes. He handed it to Romer. "You make the presentation. Give a little speech, too, how he died like a brave partigiano, that sort of thing. And make sure you get a receipt from Piero-Piero. Svenson's accountant is a maniac for receipts. He wants every penny we spend accounted for."

By nine everything was ready. Chase and Romer went outside to wait on the steps. It seemed more correct to await the partisans there than to have them ring the bell.

101

Communists, Chase knew, were very touchy about etiquette. In this respect they and D'Arcy had a lot in common.

A flight of Fiat G-50 fighters flew over. By the fasces on the wings, an emblem displaying a bundle of rods with an ax, Chase and Romer could tell they were the Italian Air Force fighting with the Germans. The planes headed south, probably on a ground support mission against Allied forces attacking the Gothic Line. The Allied offensive had begun during the night. You could hear the German artillery firing back all the way to La Spezia.

"What markings does the Italian Air Force fighting on our side use?" asked Chase.

"The rondel," said Romer. "The rondel is like the RAF's, but red-white-green. Personally, I prefer the ax. At least it's original."

"So do I," said Chase. He glanced at his watch. It was twenty past nine. "Let's hope this isn't an indication of things to come. If they're this punctual on Counter-scorch, half the town will go up before the first factory is neutralized."

"Did Svenson have anything to say about that on the cast this morning?" said Romer.

"He's waiting for a breakthrough. As soon as the Gothic Line is breached, we'll get the word. Svenson says that to go any earlier would be premature. The partisans could be flushed out before the Allies get here. It makes sense."

"Nino's brother told me the Germans would start scorching as soon as the offensive started."

"Nino's brother doesn't know what he's talking about. Why should the Germans do that? The longer they can keep the industry here working for them the better. They'll only start scorching when they know for certain that the town is lost. Which means when the Allies breach their defenses on the Gothic. As long as the Gothic holds, La Spezia is safe."

They fell silent, waiting.

"Hey, it's nine-thirty," said Kirilis, coming out the front door. "What's going on?"

"How do I know?" said Chase.

"You think they might have run into trouble?" asked Kirilis.

"They can't all have run into trouble," said Chase. "They're coming in several cars, and I doubt they're driving in a procession."

"There they are," said Kirilis as a car nosed into the driveway. "Talk about the devil. In an Alfa-Romeo, too."

"That's Szendroy's car," said Romer.

True enough, it wasn't the partisans, it was Szendroy. He pulled up beside them and got out, shoes gleaming as usual. "My friends, I have some bad news. But let us discuss them inside."

They went into the sitting room. "Before we start, would you like a coffee?" asked Chase. "It's real."

"No, thank you." He gave them a sweeping look. The air in the room was heavy with expectation. "My friends, the Allies expect to break the Gothic Line tonight."

"Hey, that's good news, not bad," said Kirilis.

"Yes, well, unfortunately . . ." Szendroy hesitated. "I received word of this on my cast from Rome, and you are to begin Counter-scorch at midnight. Unfortunately I also received a visit from a partisan with a message from Piero-Piero. He asked me to inform you they will not be coming to sign the agreement. I am to tell you they have been held up by other matters."

"So when are they coming?"

"I was not told." Szendroy gave them another all-enveloping look. "If you want my personal opinion, I don't think they will come at all. There's a rumor the Communists are preparing an uprising. If this is true, and I suspect it is, I don't think they will have any men to spare for Counter-scorch. They will put all they have into the uprising."

"In other words, they're backing out," said Chase.

"I am afraid so."

"The double-dealing bastards," Kirilis swore.

"From what I can make out," Szendroy went on, "their objective is to drive the Germans out of La Spezia before the Allies arrive. In this way they will present the Allies with a fait accompli. A Communist administration."

"What about their industry?" exclaimed Kirilis. "Don't they care for that? The moment the uprising breaks out the Germans will start pressing buttons. They're mad."

"No, they're not," said D'Arcy. "Saving industry isn't going to help them gain political power. To be sure of winning they must commit everything they have to capturing the administrative targets: post office, telephone exchange, city hall, the police stations. Those are classic revolutionary tactics. You concentrate on power, everything else is secondary."

"Any idea when the uprising is to start?" asked Chase.

"I understand it's set for tonight."

"Great," said D'Arcy. "Now what?"

"My friends, I regret to have to be the bearer of bad news. I also regret that I have to leave you. There are some friends I have to warn. If the uprising succeeds—and I understand they've infiltrated nearly ten thousand men into the city—if it succeeds, God help all those opposed to Communism. The first thing the partisans will do is to murder all their political opponents. La Spezia will have its own night of the long knives." Szendroy rose. "When is your next contact with Rome?"

"Noon," said D'Arcy.

"I would appreciate if you would inform Joe Svenson of these developments. I will try to obtain more details and give him a fuller report this evening. If by any chance I receive any good news, I will immediately telephone you. If the uprising is canceled, I will say the party is canceled. I will refer to the uprising as the party."

"You think it might be canceled?" said Romer.

104

"I don't, but one must have hope, no?"

Chase escorted Szendroy to the car. "Any news from Paola?" he asked as they stepped outside.

"They arrived safely in Genoa. My wife called me today. Cino is also there. I sent him by train to Genoa last night. I am sorry this happened. You were fond of her, no?"

"Yes, very."

"Well," he sighed, "that's how it is in these times. A bientôt."

Chase watched him drive off then walked quickly inside.

"Okay," he said, reentering the room, "so we're back to zero. We have a mission called Counter-scorch and we need troops. Any ideas on how we can carry it out now?"

"Here," said D'Arcy, handing him a plate with a glass of vodka and some black bread and caviar. "We might as well have our own celebration."

Chase held up the glass. "Gentlemen, to Counter-scorch II." He downed it in one go, blew out the fumes the way they do it in Russia, and bit on the caviar.

"We should have gone with the Badogliani from the start," said Kirilis. The Badogliani were the monarchist partisans. "Never trust a Commie."

"You would have had a hard time finding them," said Romer. "There haven't been any Badogliani in the area for months. I checked. The Communists drove them out."

"Then we should have got some from Florence or Bologna or anywhere."

"Frank, I didn't ask for regrets, I asked for suggestions," said Chase.

"What about the SOE?" said Romer. The Special Operations Executive was the British version of the OSS. "Couldn't they help?"

"They'd face the same problem we do," said D'Arcy. "Manpower."

There was a long silence as minds searched for alternatives.

"Okay," said Chase, trying to force the pace, "so the Communists are out and the Badogliani are not here. Is there any other Italian organization we can try? What about the autonomous partisans or the Mafia? There must be somebody."

"Why don't we forget about Italians? Why don't we try the Germans?" said Kirilis.

"What are you talking about?" said D'Arcy.

"In France, didn't we manage to get a president to sabotage his own factory?"

"Go on," said Chase.

"Maybe in Italy we can get the Germans to de-sabotage."

"How?"

"The same way we did it in France. Offer them a deal. Von Rota is a war criminal, isn't he?"

On the lawn of the hospital at the back of the villa a nurse was pushing a patient in a wheelchair. The patient wore a red dressing gown over a pair of pajamas. The nurse was taking him to a large oak in whose shade sat another patient in a wheelchair, this one in a blue dressing gown. The patient in blue put a monocle to his eye to observe the patient in red as he approached.

"Is that the man?" he asked.

"Yes, General," replied Silvia. "That's him." They spoke in French.

"He looks quite respectable," said von Rota in a tone of mild surprise.

"He *is* respectable, General."

"And you still won't tell me his name or what he wants?"

"I promised I wouldn't. But he will identify himself."

The general snorted. "This is the craziest caper I've taken part in since university."

The chair with the patient in red entered the shade.

"So you are in on this too, Signorina Francesca?" asked von Rota.

The nurse pushing the chair flashed him a smile. "Did you remember to take those pills?"

"Yes and they are horrible."

"But they are very effective." Francesca pressed the lever locking the chair's wheels. "And now we leave you alone. Come, Silvia."

"We will be by the fountain, General," said Silvia. "When you want me raise your arm."

The nurses left and the general surveyed Chase. "Well, young man," he said in German, "who are you and what is it that you want from me? All I know is that you speak German and that you are obviously very important to Signorina Silvia. She nearly stood on her head to get me to come here."

"Yes, Signorina Silvia can be very stubborn." Chase laughed. "Permit me to present myself, Herr General. I am Captain Chase of the American Army on a mission for General Clark."

"Are you pulling my leg, or is this serious?"

"I am not pulling your leg, Herr General."

"You are an American officer and they let you in here?" Von Rota's grey eyes scrutinized Chase.

"Let's say I let myself in," said the other.

Von Rota's eyes wandered to where Silvia and Francesca were sitting. "On second thought that doesn't really surprise me. I always suspected security in this hospital was nonexistent." He looked back at Chase. "Continue."

"As you know, Herr General, the war is coming to an end."

"*A* war," von Rota corrected. "I suspect another one will break out the moment this one ends." Like so many Germans he expected a Russo-German/American conflict to follow.

"Precisely, Herr General. And in order to win that one we must prepare now. Chancellor Bismarck was fond of

107

saying that three things are necessary to win a war: money, money, and money."

"An ancestor of mine, incidentally. Continue."

"Those industrial installations you have mined. We need them intact."

"So . . . that is why you are here."

"In return for the safekeeping of those factories we offer our protection to you and your family."

"Protection?" Von Rota started. "From what?"

"Protection from the partisans, Herr General."

"Baff!" The general snorted. "All those people are good for is terrorism, shooting soldiers in the back, ambushing ambulances, and throwing grenades into social clubs." He knew this wasn't true, but it was the sort of thing generals said, so it would sound authentic, and he wanted to draw Chase out, see what he knew of the situation, on the basis of which von Rota would be able to judge if the American was genuine.

"Not quite, Herr General. An uprising has been ordered for the second partisan zone. It will start tonight. They are committing substantial forces, drawing on units in other zones. Last night we parachuted automatic weapons and ammunition for ten thousand men. We also dropped heavy machine guns, bazookas, and artillery pieces. I am not at liberty to disclose quantities, but they have enough to take La Spezia, certainly now that your garrison is so weak."

Von Rota pondered on this in silence. It was true, the garrison was stripped to the bare minimum. The only combat troops left were the 4th Sapper, the 17th Mountain and half of the 23rd Luftwaffe; not even three battalions. Everything else was support troops. The other combat units had been sent south to bolster the front. Against ten thousand well-armed partisans the garrison wouldn't last long.

The general decided the American knew what he was talking about. Von Rota's own intelligence officer had warned him that an uprising was in the offing, confirmed by a run on salt and other staples in shops, that partisan units were infiltrating into the city, that there had been a large-scale parachute drop by American planes in the hills, that Allied commando units were operating in the hills and would probably take part in the rising.

Von Rota's mind turned to the implications of a partisan victory. He knew the partisans in the second zone were after his scalp. One of the prisoners shot in reprisal for the grenade attack on the social club was the son of the local political commissar. The partisans would show him no mercy. Aggravating the situation was the presence of his family: his wife, who was staying with him, and his son, Gunther, visiting them on leave from his unit in Denmark. The partisans wouldn't stop with him; they would murder his wife and son too. He and Patzi would end up like the military governor of Naples and his wife, hanging upside down from meat hooks.

To die like that? For what? For Hitler, that upstart who brought nothing but dishonor to the German officer corps, whose so-called military genius had resulted in a whole army being lost in Stalingrad? To die for Germany? Germany was lost. It was merely a matter of time before the Allies entered it, the question being which Allies? Von Rota guessed the country would be partitioned between the Anglo-Americans on one side and the Russians on the other. He suspected the Anglo-Americans would begin rearming Germany within a year. There was a future to live for.

He reached into a pocket of the dressing gown and brought out a silver case. "Cigarette?" he said, offering the case to Chase.

"No thank you, I don't smoke," said Chase, his eyes taking in the engraved inscription. It was signed "Canaris." A good sign, he told himself. Any friend of Canaris must be a reasonable man. Admiral Canaris, head of the Abwehr, the German military intelligence, had been

109

mixed up in the anti-Hitler opposition for most of the war.

The general lit a cigarette and inserted it into a holder. "Neutralizing those demolition charges will be more complicated than you think," he said, dragging on the cigarette.

"In what way?" asked Chase.

"The actual demolition is the task of the third and fourth companies of the sapper battalion. Both companies are SS. If I countermand the demolition order, they will immediately check with their divisional headquarters in Genoa, who will check with Berlin. After that it will only be a matter of time before I receive a visit from the local Gestapo."

"May I suggest that you follow the example of General von Stülpnagel?" said Chase. Von Stülpnagel was governor of France at the time of the putsch against Hitler. On his orders the Wehrmacht arrested the main figures in the SS and Gestapo.

"Von Stülpnagel paid with his life for that caper," replied von Rota. For his part in the failed putsch, von Stülpnagel was hanged.

"Herr General, there are always risks," said Chase.

"Yes, that's true," said von Rota pensively. He took another drag on his cigarette. "Before I decide which risk to choose, perhaps you would explain how you propose to assure the safety of myself and my family."

"By making sure that the uprising fails, Herr General."

"How can you do that? You said yourself they have enough men and material to take La Spezia."

"I said with the garrison as weak as it is. But if the garrison were reinforced . . ." He let the word hang.

"There's nothing to reinforce it with. Everything is at the front."

"The situation at the front could change, Herr General, the way it did when the Warsaw rising broke out."

A look of stupefaction appeared on von Rota's face. He knew the Americans were not the angels they made

110

themselves out to be, but could they, too, be so Machiavellic?

"General Clark is prepared to do a Rokossovsky?" he asked.

Chase nodded. "Those industries are very important to us."

In the summer of 1944, as the Red Army's offensive neared Warsaw, an uprising broke out in the city. Organized by the Polish underground, it was, like so many risings in World War II, a double-edged operation. Militarily it was aimed at the enemy, politically at the ally. In Poland, the Russian ally made no secret of his intention to turn the country into a Communist state, just as in Greece the British ally was making sure the country remained a monarchy. As soon as an area of Poland was liberated, the underground administration was arrested and replaced by Russian protégés. The mayor's seat, vacated by the German governor, was not filled by the underground's candidate, but by a Polish Communist trained in Moscow. It was to prevent this from happening in the capital that the rising was organized. If the capital could be in Polish hands before the arrival of the Russians, the country might still be saved.

To liquidate mayors, police chiefs, and partisans in the provinces was not too difficult. It could be done quietly at night, under the guise of eliminating Fascist elements. There were no international observers in the provinces. But there would be in Warsaw. As soon as the capital was in Polish hands, planes would be landing with war correspondents, Allied missions, military and diplomatic, Red Cross, UNRA, not to mention elements of the Polish Army in England, which were on standby for this purpose. To eliminate the underground administration in Warsaw would take a lot of shooting. The best partisan units were there, totalling some fifty thousand men, and Warsaw was

111

not Vilna. It had a population of a million people. And then could one permit oneself the international scandal that would follow if a city, which with its own hands had thrown out the invader, was subsequently subjected to a siege by an ally, a scandal that would inevitably have repercussions on Russia's Anglo-American allies? The Poles calculated that one couldn't, and so they prepared to gamble. A gamble it was, for if the uprising failed, the cream of the nation would go down with it and the Communist subjugation of the country would be even easier than if the uprising had never occurred. As with all uprisings, the trick was to time it right; not too early otherwise the enemy, still strong, could quash it, but early enough for the insurrectionists to control the town before the arrival of the liberators.

All this General Rokossovsky was aware of as he plotted the Russian countermove to the Polish gamble. A first-rate chess player, Rokossovsky knew the value of drawing out the opponent. He decided to draw out the Poles. As his artillery pounded German positions on the outskirts of Warsaw, as his Yak fighters fought dogfights over the city, as the town's patriots burned with desire for action, Rokossovsky had Radio Moscow broadcast an appeal: to the citizens of Warsaw . . . the hour has struck . . . arise . . . help the Red Army throw out the invader. The underground rose to the bait. Within twenty-four hours the uprising was in full swing. Which is when Rokossovsky halted his offensive. The artillery fell silent, Russian Yaks disappeared from the sky to be replaced by German Stuka dive bombers, Russian troops left their trenches to sunbathe on the banks of the Vistula. Taking advantage of the lull, the Germans brought back one division after another to quell the rising. It took them two months to do it, in the course of which the underground army was decimated, a quarter-million civilians killed, and after the rest had been evacuated the town razed to the ground like Carthage. When the Russians resumed their offensive there wasn't even a Battle of Warsaw. There was no Warsaw. The country was without a capital, headless, leaderless, hopeless, ready to accept Communism without a squeak. General Rokossovsky was promoted to Marshal and a term was added to the military jargon of World War II: "To do a Rokossovsky."

"Which is what we're going to do to Piero-Piero and Co.," said Chase, ending his briefing to the Boxers.

"Will Clark agree to halt the offensive?" asked D'Arcy.

"That's what we have to have confirmed," said Chase.

"Of course he'll agree," said Kirilis. "In those regions they all scratch each other's backs. Clark will save Kramer, after the war Kramer will give Clark a job, then Clark will use his contacts in the military to get contracts for Kramer."

"The next cast is at five," said D'Arcy. "We'll have to transmit on Szendroy's set. There's something wrong with ours. I still haven't located the fault."

Chase glanced at his watch. "If we have to do it at Szendroy's, we'd better go now. Do we have a car?"

Romer nodded. "A Fiat Balila. I rented it from the hotel manager. False license plates."

"Okay, Jeff, let's go."

They drove to Szendroy's art gallery. Besides his main gallery in Genoa, he kept two smaller ones, one in La Spezia, the other in Savona. On the way Chase said, "What's bugging Frank? He seems very 'anti' on the mission."

"He doesn't like our fighting to defend the interests of the rich."

"What has he got against the rich?"

"Frank considers all the rich to be capitalist exploiters. I think it's a reaction to his family. The grandfather made a fortune on the back of Russian peasants, the father made his from sick Greek immigrants. I suppose you know that Frank's father is a doctor."

"Yes, I know that."

"I gather he's no Schweitzer. To hear Frank talk, the father charges his patients for the smallest service and threatens to have them deported if they don't pay their bills. Frank thinks it's wrong that a doctor should make a fortune from sick people. The example of his father has turned Frank into a champion of the underdog. Actually in your presence he's relatively subdued, but you should hear him when he gets going on the subject of capitalist exploiters and workers' rights. He sounds like a founding father of the Socialist International."

"Is he a socialist?"

"Not politically, but socially, yes, if you get me. When I was last Stateside I met a guy who worked with him at Fent Chemicals before the war. Another chemical engineer. You should have heard the way he talked about Frank."

"What, knocking him?"

"No, singing his praises. Apparently Frank held a very important post there, he was head of a department in the mining explosives division. This guy said Frank was the most popular department head in the company. Among the workers, that is. The directors thought he was pinko. Apparently there was a queue of people wanting to be transferred to Frank's department. This guy said Frank had a reputation as a boss who treated his employees not as machines but as human beings." D'Arcy swerved to avoid a man on a bicycle who shot out of a side street, a school satchel on his back. "I bet that's a partisan courier." The man was well past school age. "He's an amazing man, Frank. There's an aura about him of a playboy and ever so often you catch a glimpse that makes you realize the playboy part is just a facade."

"What I like about him is that he doesn't take himself seriously. Did I ever tell you what he told me when I was interviewing him for the group? I asked him why he wanted to be the demolition man. He replied—"

"That he liked blowing things up. You told me."

114

"Did I? I'm beginning to repeat myself. Must be age."

They pulled up before the art gallery. Szendroy was in the back office with a customer, so they looked at pictures while waiting. There was an exhibition of watercolors by an up and coming fascist artist. There were paintings showing men at war in heroic poses, there were sturdy foundry workers, there were workers building tanks, there were paintings glorifying motherhood and there were even paintings glorifying the barrack apartments on the way to the industrial park.

"Socialismus-realismus," said D'Arcy.

The customer went away and they went in Szendroy's office. Chase gave him a report on his meeting with von Rota.

"Glänzend!" exclaimed Szendroy. Like so many Hungarians of his class, he expressed emotion in German, a practice dating back to the days of the Austro-Hungarian empire when that was the chic thing to do.

"Let's not cry hop, Henrik," said D'Arcy. "Clark may not go for it."

"Did not Svenson approve your approach?"

"Svenson did, but in turn he has to have approval from Clark," said Chase.

They told Szendroy about their radio problems, so he led them upstairs to an apartment above the gallery—a pied à terre he once used for sleeping with his mistresses but which now was used exclusively for radio transmissions. From under the floorboards he brought the radio set and a car battery, gave Chase pencil and paper, and went back to look after his shop. While D'Arcy strung the antenna and the ground wire, Chase wrote out the message, then coded it. For coding the Boxers used the Onetime Pad method. It comprised two pads with similar pages. On each page was a different code. One of the pads was with the Boxers, the other in Rome. To indicate which code you were using you simply gave the number of the page. You used one page per message. That way if the enemy broke a code he could only decode that particular message. The information he gained from breaking the code would be useless to him for future casts because the pages used different systems of coding.

When he finished encoding, Chase took the original draft and the coding page to the kitchen and burned them in the sink, flushing the ashes down the drain. This way if the Gestapo were to burst in on them during transmission they would have no way of telling what was being transmitted. What D'Arcy had was several pages filled with columns of letters. That was why the Gestapo were unable to learn the contents of the message Paola sent to Rome the night they captured her, a message that dealt with Counter-scorch.

"How is this deal going to work?" asked D'Arcy, lighting a cigarette and sitting down. Everything was ready, there was nothing to do except wait. "I'd like to know in case I have to ask Rome for emergency frequencies."

"Okay, let's assume that by now Svenson has received Clark's approval," said Chase. "He tells us that in his reply. At which time he will also tell us what color pattern our side will use to signal the halt of the offensive. The Germans have to know that the lull is permanent before they start withdrawing troops. So then I go to von Rota and I tell him to inform General von Palten—he commands their Ligurian sector—that the ceasefire will be signaled by our artillery firing red shells followed by a salvo of green, followed by a salvo of yellow, let's say. After I see von Rota, I return to the villa where we drink the vodka and wait. Von Rota will call us as soon as the uprising breaks out. We message Rome—we'd better take Szendroy's set with us—Rome messages our front line, we cease fire, von Rota countermands the demolition order. After that we play it by ear."

D'Arcy smoked in silence, mulling this over. "Who's commanding our side of the Ligurian sector?"

"A General Depuis. Why?"

"I find the communication setup too complicated. We message Rome, Rome messages Depuis, he comes back to Rome. That's nice in theory but in practice there are delays, messages get lost, the whole thing could take hours. What if we need to communicate with him in a hurry? On a deal like this a thousand and one things could go wrong. An accidental discharge, and before you know it the shooting starts all over again. If we want to make sure the ceasefire works, we need direct contact with Depuis."

"How do you suggest we do that?"

"Ask Rome to assign an OSS liaison officer to Depuis' HQ. Preferably with his own radio. They can fly him in tonight. Between the liaison officer and us we'll establish a direct link and keep it open twenty-four hours a day. That way if any problems arise they can be dealt with immediately. We could even take one of our sets and install it in von Rota's HQ. Dispense with phone calls. We might even have to do that if the partisans capture the telephone exchange."

Chase considered the other's proposition. "Okay, let's ask Rome for a liaison officer," he said finally. He wrote out another message, coded it, and destroyed the original and the code. Then he went to D/F watch.

Normally, D/F watching was done from a window that enabled one to see both ends of a street, but Szendroy's apartment did not have a window facing the street so Chase had to D/F watch from the street. As it happened there was an ideal spot. On the other side of the street was a café bar with two tables on the sidewalk. Chase took one of the tables and ordered a mineral water and a newspaper. While the waiter went to fetch his order, Chase inspected the street. It was narrow and short and empty, the kind of street where he would notice any suspicious characters right away, such as men with up-turned collars and pulled-down hats hiding earphones

117

connected to D/F apparatus under the coat. The last few streets of a D/F operation were usually done on foot. A van gave the show away.

The waiter brought him his order. Chase paid and opened the newspaper. Italy was winning the war, Germany was winning the war, Japan was winning the war. Milan beat Turin at football. Bandits robbed a postal van. The duchess of so-and-so had died. City hall voted credit to replant the trees on Via Garibaldi, which were dying from a mysterious tree disease. He glanced left and right. The street was empty. He turned to a critique of a play by Pirandello that had opened the previous night at the municipal theatre. At that moment three men in suits and felt hats walked out of the café.

"Your papers," said one of them, flashing a Carabinieri plaque.

Chase handed him his passport, his mind whirling. They must have been inside checking papers. But why? Did it have anything to do with the art gallery? Was the gallery under observation? Or was it coincidence? Could they be checking IDs in connection with something totally different? But what? Uprising? "Are you searching for those robbers who robbed the postal van?" he asked casually.

"Nothing to do with that," replied the man. He turned to the others. "A foreigner."

The other shrugged his shoulders. "Book him."

The first man closed the passport. "Please come with us, sir."

"I don't understand," said Chase, feigning confusion. "What have I done?"

"A simple formality, sir. Enemy agents are reported in town and we have orders to pick up anyone who is not from La Spezia."

They walked to a small police van parked round a corner, Chase scanning the surroundings for an avenue of escape. But he couldn't see anything. On top of which he was virtually surrounded, two men on either side of him, one behind. By the time he reached the nearest alley he'd be dead. The back of the van with its grilled window drew closer and closer. Chase prayed for that moment when he would see something and his instinct would say, Now! But nothing came. Perspiration broke out on his forehead. What was wrong? he asked himself. Was he getting old? Had he lost his touch? This had never happened to him, this drying up of his imagination. What was it, lack of energy? And yet he had had an early night. He couldn't believe it, he was going into captivity. *Clang!* The door closed behind him. And there he was, the famous Boxer, a rabbit in a cage.

The inspector behind the desk flipped through the passport for the second time. He was a small man with glossy hair and squinting eyes. A strong smell of lotion and pomade exuded from his person. He struck Chase as a typical police bureaucrat: not stupid, not clever, provincial, and easily impressed by a traveler from the land of bolas and the tango. While the inspector went through the passport, studying the various visas, Chase's eyes traveled from the portrait of Mussolini on the wall behind the inspector to the framed quotation from Mussolini on the right wall: "Better to live one day as a lion than fifty years as a sheep." Chase wondered if the inspector considered he was now living like a lion.

"What kind of a name is Bosch?" asked the inspector. "It's not Spanish."

"German," replied Chase. "My father was German. He emigrated to Argentina, where he met my mother. My mother is Italian."

The inspector nodded. "I was asking myself how you came to speak such good Italian." His face took on a pensive look. "If your father was German does not that mean you have German nationality?"

"Yes, I have dual nationality."

119

The inspector flipped through more pages. The various visas seemed to fascinate him. "What brings you to La Spezia?"

"We had a free day in Genoa. Someone suggested that La Spezia was worth a visit." They had gone over the economic mission already.

"Where are you staying?"

"I am not. I arrived this morning and I am leaving this evening for Genoa. By train."

The inspector closed the passport. "Do you know the city of Rosario in Argentina?"

"Very well, I've been to it many times."

"I have a brother there. He wants me to join him. He says he can get me a job with the local police. The money is good. But I don't speak Spanish."

"That won't be a problem," Chase assured him. "For an Italian, Spanish is easy. Two or three months and you'll be speaking it well enough to work. You should go. It's a great country. My father used to say coming to Argentina was the best thing he did."

The inspector nodded, tapping the passport with his hand. Finally he said, "As far as I am concerned you're free to go. But because you have German nationality we'll have to have you cleared by our German colleagues. A formality that won't take long. I'll take you to them."

Chase followed him along a corridor crowded with men picked off the streets. They were waiting to be interrogated by other inspectors in offices on each side of the corridor. Many of them seemed to know each other. The air was noisy and thick with smoke. Through the open office doors, Chase could see interrogations in progress, arguments accompanied by shouting and hand waving. It was typical Italy, bubbly, full of life. At each end of the corridor, guarding the gathering, stood two Carabinieri armed with machine pistols. To Chase it was clear that the roundup had the uprising in mind. Contrary to what the man who picked him up said, the roundup was not limited to

120

foreigners. There were people of all walks of life in the corridor, picked up probably because their papers were not in order, meaning they might be without a tobacco ration card or their discharge papers, absences that usually indicated partisans.

Just before the end of the corridor, the inspector stopped at a door marked Geheime Staatspolizei. He knocked and they entered. It was like going into a different world. In place of the smoke and the noise was a quiet businesslike atmosphere underlined by the subdued clatter of teletypes. The place was clean, the air unpolluted. At a T-shaped table sat three young men, handsome in their black uniforms with swastika armbands. They had pistols strapped to their belts. Two were typing, one was reading a newspaper. They looked bright, efficient. The inspector went up to one of them and spoke with the deference Chase had observed so often among conquered people. The other replied with a few energetic nods and went through an unmarked door. He came out shortly, bid the other enter, and motioned Chase to a bench.

Chase sat down, his mind preparing itself for the interview. There were two possibilities, he decided. The Germans would treat him as a formality and he had nothing to worry about. Or they might decide to check, in which case he was in a real pickle, for with the Italian he had deviated from his cover. The Boxers' cover was that they had arrived in La Spezia from Milan for a few days' rest prior to going on to Genoa. It was a solid cover in the sense that if the authorities wanted to check, Chase could give them names and telephone numbers of people who would corroborate it. What made him decide to deviate from the cover was that if he stuck to it he would have to give the address of the villa. That would mean involving the other Boxers at a critical moment in their mission. Let's say the police booked them all for the night while they checked. Who would act as liaison between von Rota and Depuis? Or the police might find out in the course of the interview that neither D'Arcy nor Kirilis spoke Spanish. With Romer and him it was different; they could communicate with authorities in their own language. Then there was the chance that while the police were at the villa D'Arcy could arrive with a radio. By changing the cover Chase had taken the risk on himself, assuring that the presence of the others remained a secret.

The inspector came out, minus Chase's passport. "Inspector Platz will see you shortly," he told Chase. He held out his hand. "Goodbye. Maybe we'll see each other in Argentina one day."

"I hope so," said Chase. "Goodbye."

He resumed his seat and waited. Five minutes went by. Ten. Twenty. Chase's blood pressure began going up. This sort of treatment boded no good. Then the telephone rang. One of the men spoke into it briefly and came up to Chase.

"Inspector Platz will see you. This way, please."

The office he led him into was unusual. There was an Oriental carpet, the furniture was more the kind one sees in a sitting room rather than an office, the light was subdued, there were plants. Behind a Louis XV desk sat a woman wearing a black uniform, white shirt, and tie. She too had a red-white-and-black swastika armband. Like the men in the office she was good looking, but while their looks were cliché—blond blue-eyed Aryans—her looks had character. In the first place, she was not a blond but a brunette. Her hair was jet black, as were her eyes. In the second, her skin was not Nordic milk but freckled. Very freckled. The freckles distracted the eye from the well-shaped face so that at first the face seemed merely interesting. Only with time did one realize that the interesting face was also handsome. It was a face that grew on you. He judged her to be in her late twenties.

"Nehmen Sie Platz, bitte." She motioned him to one

of the chairs facing the desk. "You do speak German, don't you?"

"Yes, I do," he replied, sitting down. By the look she gave him he could tell she welcomed this handsome distraction from the tedium of routine. Chase guessed she belonged to the documentation section, where they often employed women, doing liaison work with Italians, rather than to the investigative side, although she probably did a bit of that, too, as these things tended to overlap.

"I understand from Inspector Prestini that you are a German national," she said, picking up his passport.

"Yes, I am," he replied. "My father was German."

"In Italy, nonmilitary German nationals are under the joint jurisdiction of Italian and German authorities. I regret to have to put you through this, but you will have to tell your story to me again."

So Chase retold his story.

When he had finished, she said, "I understand you are here only for a day?"

"Yes, I am returning to Genoa on the train tonight."

"May I see your train ticket?"

Gott im Himmel! Chase's mind whirled. He lost it. No, that wouldn't do. People didn't lose train tickets. "I only bought a one-way ticket and I threw the stub away." It was the next best thing that came into his head. Even as he said it, though, he felt it sounded phony.

She, however, seemed to accept it at face value. Maybe she wasn't very experienced, he said to himself. "Where are you staying in Genoa?"

"The Colombia-Excelsior," he replied. He knew the hotel from a prewar trip to Genoa with his father.

She picked up the phone. "Connect me with the Colombia-Excelsior in Genoa." She scanned the pad, on which she made notes while he told his story. "You said you arrived in Genoa aboard the *Iberian Star*."

"Yes."

"May I see your ship ticket?"

"I am afraid I don't have it with me. I left it in my hotel room."

"I see." She gave the notes another perusal. "Besides your passport, have you any other identification?"

Chase brought out his wallet. He handed her his Buenos Aires driving license, his medical insurance card, two club membership cards, and a library card.

She took down the particulars and handed them back to him. Then the telephone rang. "Yes?" There was a pause. "That long? Well, keep trying." She put the receiver down. "There's a half-hour delay on calls to Genoa, so I must ask you to be patient. Would you like some coffee?"

"With pleasure," said Chase.

She picked up the phone and ordered coffee for both of them. She glanced back at the pad. "When did your father emigrate to Argentina?"

There followed a question and answer period about the Bosch family in Argentina. None of it had much to do with confirmation of his identity—they were hardly going to phone Argentina to see if he was telling the truth—but Chase guessed that wasn't the purpose. The purpose was to compile information on people of German extraction who might be useful to the Gestapo at some future date. For instance, Chase's "brother" was an officer in the Argentinian Navy. One of Chase's "sisters" was married to a banker, also of German extraction. Next she pumped him about the economic mission, what it hoped to accomplish, the trade picture between Argentina and Italy, information of little value to his identity but useful economic intelligence.

Under normal circumstances the trend of the conversation would have been encouraging, would have pleased him, for it showed she believed he was Bosch, a German-Argentinian on an economic mission. On this occasion, however, that was little comfort. Sooner or later that telephone would ring and the cat would be out of the bag that there was no Bosch at the Colombia-Excelsior. The only hope was that the call would never get through, that delay would follow delay. There was always a possibility that the line might be booked solid with priority calls, one reason why he was engaging in this charade. Another was that the longer he delayed telling her the truth, the longer it would be before she sent him to the Gestapo station. If the uprising broke out before he was transferred, he might be saved. There was a good chance that the partisans would capture the Italian station. Capturing the Gestapo one would be much harder. The Gestapo would fight like lions.

The arrival of the coffee brought the interview to a halt. They had more or less covered all there was to cover anyway. The mood changed. The inspector became the charming hostess who pours coffee for her guest. It had arrived on a trolley, wheeled in by one of the blue-eyed blonds from the front.

"You have a very nice office," said Chase, glancing around. "I like your plants."

"I spend a great deal of time in here, so I have tried to make it more like a home. We're very short staffed."

Chase's eyes traveled to a photo in a silver frame on a shelf of the bookcase. It was the picture of the inspector with a man and two small boys. "Are those your children?"

"Yes," she said, bringing him his coffee. "My sons. They were killed in an air raid on Hamburg. We lived in Hamburg. My husband was also killed in it."

"I am sorry," said Chase.

"That's war." She sighed sadly, eyes on the photo. "Excuse me," she said, noticing her distraction. She held out the sugar bowl and he helped himself to it. "Are you married?" she asked.

"No, I am not."

The telephone rang. "Pronto," she said, raising her

voice the way people do when talking long distance. "This is the German police in La Spezia." She spoke Italian with a slight trace of German accent. To Chase the combination was very sexy. She had a nice voice anyway. "I would like confirmation of a registration there. The name is Karl Bosch." She spelled the name. "He is part of an Argentinian economic mission. Argentinian," she repeated. "Yes, from Buenos Aires. One moment." She cupped the mouthpiece. "When did you register?"

"On the tenth," said Chase, choosing a date at random.

"On the tenth," she repeated into the telephone. "Pronto, are you there? Pronto." She tapped the switch. "Oh, no!" she exclaimed. She tapped the switch some more. "We've been cut off," she said for Chase's benefit. She replaced the receiver and lifted it again. "Connect me again to the Colombia-Excelsior in Genoa. I was cut off."

It was a good half hour before she got the connection again. They spent it chatting about this and that, two civilized people versed in the art of conversation passing time in an interesting way, getting to know each other, getting to like each other. He told her about Argentina and the United States—she had relatives in Boston—she told him about Italy and Germany. In the process he learned that she had studied languages at the University of Göttingen, that in addition to Italian she spoke English and French, that her husband was a fighter pilot, that after her family was wiped out she decided to go to work and saw a Gestapo advertisement for linguists, that she only took over the job from her boss a month earlier, he having been killed in an ambush by partisans.

One reason Chase learned so much about her was that he was good at getting people to talk, especially women. He had the ability to give the impression that he found them fascinating. With her he outdid himself because as long as she talked, he didn't have to talk about himself. He didn't want to lie to her about himself. He didn't mind

126

lying to her about the economic mission and the Bosch family. That was part of his job, she would understand that. But to shoot her a line about his personal life after she had opened herself to him about hers struck him as inelegant. In this respect Chase resembled a man about to face a firing squad. At such moments values undergo a change. The important thing becomes not life, since you're as good as dead; the important thing becomes to die well. For all he knew she might be the last human to see him alive—after her it would be the animals—and he would like her to remember him not as an out-and-out liar who made a fool of her, but as a gentleman who was forced to lie in the line of duty. When he made his exit, he wanted to do it with dignity.

The telephone rang. "Yes?" she said. "Yes, we were cut off." There was a long pause. "Are you sure?" she asked, her eyes avoiding Chase's. "Hold on." She cupped the receiver. "What is your room number?" All of a sudden the tone was distant, official.

"Hang up."

She started. "I beg your pardon?"

"You don't know the room number. Thank him and hang up," he ordered her.

A confused expression crossed her face, the look of a woman who suddenly feels very much a woman and not an inspector. The authority in his voice, the way he took the initiative, rattled her. For a moment she felt as if she were in his chair and he behind the desk. But she recovered. "We don't have the number, but thank you for the information." She replaced the receiver and leaned back in her chair, looking down at the hands in her lap. Then she looked at him and held his eyes. "You know what this means, don't you?" she asked sadly.

Chase nodded. "You pass me to the muscle boys."

"Who are you?"

"I can't tell you."

"Are you an Allied agent?"

"Something like that." He watched her eyes probe his face as if she were trying to remember it before the muscle boys turned it to pulp. It was clear she was genuinely sorry, even upset, that she would have to turn him over. "Don't look so sad." He smiled. "As you said, that's war." He saw her flinch and immediately regretted having said it, for the implication was that what the Allied bombers had done to her was no different from from what she was doing to him. He regretted it because if there was one person who did not deserve a dagger plunged into her heart, it was her. By equating the two actions he was crushing her, robbing her of her self-pity, the self-pity that was necessary to carry her through her grief. Now she would never again be able to say "That's war" in a tone that invited sympathy. Now if she wanted to be true to herself she would have to say it in a way that indicated she dished out as well as she got. But the damage was done, and he could think of nothing that would repair it. "You'd better call them," he said with a nod at the telephone. "But first tell me your name."

"Gudrun," she said softly, eyes on the hands in her lap. She glanced at the ceiling. "To think," she sighed, "the number of times they told us, 'Don't . . .'" She let the words hang.

". . . get involved," said Chase, finishing it for her. He smiled. "Only shows you're human after all."

She looked at him sadly. "And you? What is your name?"

"I don't have one," he said coldly.

She nodded to herself, looking away, then leaned and picked up the receiver. "Connect me with headquarters."

The room was in darkness except for a low-hanging ceiling lamp with a large shade. It illuminated a table at which sat a thick-set man with a bald head that exuded force. He was dressed in a double-breasted suit, and there was a flower in his lapel. The man had thick lips and a fleshy jowl, and his eyes said he could probably mind-read. He was smoking a cigarette, tapping it occasionally against a large glass ashtray while studying a file. By one of the walls sat a group of men, their burning cigarette ends glowing in the dark. They were silent and the air was heavy with expectation. Chase, his hands handcuffed before him, stood facing the table, flanked by two guards with rubber truncheons.

So this is how it was in real life, he reflected. He had to admit it was a vast improvement over what went on during training at the Farm in Virginia. To begin with, the waiting heightened tension, gave a sense of drama. In Virginia, they went to work on you right away, the moment you stepped through the door. In Virginia, too, the interrogator wore fatigues. Here not only did he wear a suit with a flower, he was freshly shaven. A nice touch, that, thought Chase. It made you feel really special. Finally, in Virginia the interrogator was flanked by two assistants, here he was alone . . . but with an audience. Altogether you could tell you were in a different league.

"Sit down."

One of the guards prodded him with a truncheon and he took the lone chair facing the table. For some reason, now that he was in the circle of light, he was much more conscious of the presence of the gorillas behind him. He felt his palms becoming moist and his throat parch. That, too, was part of the real thing, he reflected, something you weren't taught during training. As long as you were standing in the dark, out of the reach of the light, you could observe, feel a certain detachment, like a spectator watching a lit stage. The moment you entered the circle of light, however, the perspective changed. You became the play.

The fact that he was capable of such esoteric thoughts at such a critical time surprised him. He had expected

129

his mind would be paralyzed with fear, incapable of thought, as they told you at the Farm. Instead, he could think clearly. His mind was lucid. He attributed this to the hour he spent in the cell waiting for the interrogation. It gave him time to arrange his thoughts to select a course of action, and once he had selected it to come to terms with its outcome. This is why he wasn't nervous, why he could think: there was nothing to be nervous about. He knew what was coming. By deciding to plead guilty he had done away with chance. He, not chance, was guiding his destiny. The thought pleased him, for Chase liked to think of himself as a man who does not allow himself to be led by the nose by fate, but as a man who shapes it. That he would pay for this privilege dearly was secondary. What counted was the satisfaction that even before the interrogation had begun he had grasped the initiative. By selecting to plead guilty, he had decided how the interrogation would go.

In OSS jargon pleading guilty meant you admitted to being an agent but refused to divulge the purpose of your mission. You simply clammed up, took your punishment like a good boy, and when they got tired of beating you went off to a concentration camp or to the firing wall. Cases of people pleading guilty were rare. They either took the "L" tablet before they got anywhere near the interrogation room, or they pleaded not guilty. To plead not guilty meant you either stuck by your cover, cost be what it may, or you invented a new one. For example, an agent might claim to be a downed airman, or one caught with a transmitter might claim he met this guy by chance who wanted a suitcase taken from A to B.

Before making his decision in the cell, Chase had in fact considered trying the route of another cover. The most promising was to present himself as an American officer belonging to G-2 of the 92nd Division who had been infiltrated through enemy lines to La Spezia, his mission being to enter into contact with the partisans in order to coordinate joint military action. It was the most promising in the sense that it was the most plausible; the situation at the front, the planned uprising, made such an initiative on the part of the commander of the 92nd natural. The problem was how did one square such a cover with the possession of a Buenos Aires driving license and medical insurance plan? No G-2 would think of going to those lengths for what was basically a very simple and frequent undercover operation. Officers were being infiltrated behind enemy lines all the time. Then there were other holes that had emerged in the course of an imaginary conversation he held with his interrogator in the cell:

How did you get to La Spezia?

I walked.

Where did you sleep?

In caves. This way the interrogator couldn't prove him wrong. He could have if Chase said he stayed at people's homes. The interrogator would ask for addresses.

Where's your gear?

I came as is.

You walked four days in this suit?

Yes.

You slept in caves, shaved in streams and folded your suit nicely before going to sleep, right?

Right.

You forgot something.

What?

You also had an iron.

What do you mean?

Look at your shirt, it's freshly pressed.

Whack! Down would come the rubber truncheon.

In the course of his analysis in the cell Chase had decided he would be beaten sooner or later. The choice, aside from the philosophical considerations, boiled down to pleading quilty and being beaten right away or pleading not guilty and being beaten later. The latter had an obvious advantage, it postponed pain. Offsetting it, however, was the moral disadvantage. To plead not guilty meant you had to lie, it meant having to listen to the interrogator call you a lying swine, once he caught you out, insinuate that you were a worm who did not have the courage to stand up like a man, tell the truth, and collect his due. It meant having to hear some unpleasant truths about yourself because the fact was you were a liar. That lowered your morale. The other route raised your morale. A man who clams up from the beginning has righteousness on his side. He will get beaten as much as a liar but at least when it's all over, he can come out walking tall, as they say in cowboy land. Far from being a worm, he is a patriot, a hero, perhaps even a saint. To go down as a hero was much more Chase's style.

"Well, now," said the interrogator, closing the file. He stubbed out the cigarette and pushed the ashtray to the side. He leaned with his arms on the table, hands clasped, and gave Chase a penetrating look. "Tell us about yourself."

It took all of Chase's willpower to fight down the temptation to take the other route, to postpone if only by a few minutes the pain that would follow. He replied, "I have nothing to say." He had the impression someone else was talking through his mouth.

"Really?" said the interrogator, feigning surprise. "You have nothing to say. Why is that, I wonder? Don't you like us?" His voice hardened ominously. "Or is it that you have something to hide?"

"I have nothing to say."

A deadly hush fell over the room. The interrogator stared at Chase, his mind-reading eyes boring into him. He looked down at his hands and said, "Perhaps I should explain. I am Inspector Schumacher and behind you are Detectives Fuchs and Zuben. We are professionals. We have a reputation for never letting a man out of our clutches without getting the truth from him. It might take us a day, it might take two days, it might take us three. But eventually we get it out. We have been in this business a long time. We know exactly how much pain to inflict so it hurts but doesn't kill. We don't afford our victims the luxury of death. No one has ever left us dead. Mad, yes. But not dead. I am saying this because from time to time people come to us with misconceptions. Somewhere along the line they have picked up the erroneous notion that after the first few blows the nervous system becomes numb and death takes care of the rest. This may be so in other stations, but not here. Now then, let's begin again. What is your name?"

"I have nothing to say," said Chase, bracing himself for the blow that would follow. Romer described it as an experience similar to a dentist's drill striking a nerve, except that it was multiplied over the entire nervous system. But Chase wasn't thinking of that. He was concentrating on something else Romer had said. Romer said that a man's moral education was not complete until he had been tortured. Romer could talk with authority on the matter, for of the four he was the only one who had been tortured. Now Chase would be the second. A man's education is not complete until he undergoes torture. A man's education is not complete . . . Chase repeated the phrase over and over, waiting for the blow. Instead he heard the interrogator say, "You think we will beat you, don't you? We won't. That's messy. People who are beaten tend to be sick. We don't like mess around here. We have more refined ways of making people want to talk to us. Have you heard of the gé-gène?" Chase's blood froze. "We like calling it by its French name. So much more descriptive, don't you think? Or don't you speak French? Perhaps you haven't heard of it either. In which case I'll let you in on a secret." He lowered his voice. "Prolonged exposure imperils the ability to do it with girls. You get my point? Keep it in mind," he added paternally. He

133

raised his eyes above Chase's head. "Gentlemen, please do the honors."

A light switch clicked and a wall lit up, an empty white wall, lit like a background in a photographer's studio. A hand tugged him by the collar. They led him to a table, undid his handcuffs and began to undress him. They did it without hurrying, without hurting, in fact there was almost a certain softness in their movements. Chase was reminded of a day in New Jersey. Driving along the highway with his mother, they saw a sign that ducks were for sale. His mother asked him to drive in and buy one. Chase watched the farmer kill it. What he remembered about the scene most was not the killing but the unhurried, gentle, almost considerate way in which the farmer handled the duck. In a way, these men made him feel like that duck.

As they got to his socks, another thought occurred to him, that he was being very submissive, like those Nationalist prisoners in the Spanish Civil War being marched to their execution by the Republicans. He had seen a picture in a magazine. He remembered thinking at the time it was strange that people allowed themselves to be taken to their doom so placidly. Why didn't they strike out? Why didn't they take one of the guards with them? Now he knew why. To start a punchup seemed not only undignified but juvenile. So you might hurt one of them. You might even kill one of them. So what? It wouldn't change your lot. On top of which it was impossible to be in two frames of mind at once: preparing yourself for death or torture and at the same time preparing to fight. In his case he could see himself turning on them if they hurt him, if they were rough. But they weren't. He didn't even feel hostile to them. In their own way, he thought, they were probably quite nice people, kind to their children, considerate of their parents. Here they were simply doing their job. He was a mystery, their job was to unravel the mystery, get him to talk. The pain was incidental.

134

When he was completely naked they gave him an empty jam jar and told him to urinate into it. They didn't want him to do it on the floor. They led him to the lit wall and attached his hands with handcuffs to a rail running above. To do that they had to climb on a chair. When they had attached him, he was on his toes. Then they left him. The lights burned into his eyes. He couldn't see anything in the room, not even the interrogator's lamp. But he heard a lot of scraping as if they were moving equipment. Soon one of the guards returned holding wires at the end of which were clamps. He attached one clamp to Chase's genitals, the other to his ear, and left. He came back with a wet towel and dabbed both clamps. It would improve conductivity. Taking the chair with him he disappeared into the dark and a hush settled over the room. The voice of the interrogator boomed:

"Your name and rank."

Chase said nothing.

"I am awaiting your answer," the interrogator called.

"I have nothing to say," Chase replied.

There was the whirl of a hand-pedaled generator and electricity seared through his body, shaking him like a leaf, deforming his face, contorting his muscles. Scream after scream rent the room, the handcuffs rattling against the railing in a macabre dance. He was like a puppet.

The whirling stopped, leaving him gasping for air. The electricity had prevented him from breathing. Every muscle in his body was on fire and there was an excruciating pain in his testicles. Bit by bit his vision returned. He was covered in sweat and began shaking from the cold.

Out of the darkness the interrogator's voice informed him:

"I should tell you that the pain will get worse as time progresses. Every shock lowers the body's resistance, making it that much more sensitive. Remember what I told you, we never let a man leave us without getting the truth out of him. Now then, your name and rank."

Chase said nothing, all his being concentrating on a phrase turning in his mind like a broken record: a man's moral education is not complete until he has undergone torture. This is good for you. This is to be welcomed. It will make you a better person. It will keep you human, it will keep you human, it will keep you human.

"Answer me!"

Chase felt tears enter his eyes. He felt so very lonely. And he was so terribly cold.

"I am awaiting your answer."

"I have nothing to say!" he cried in anger.

The generator whirled and more screams rent the room. The torture went on for another four question-and-answer sessions before mercifully his body gave out and he was dragged out of the room unconscious.

When he came to he was in his cell. A semicircle of faces peered down at him from under steel helmets. The men wore black leather coats and carried arms. A panic seized him. An SS firing squad. They had come to get him. They were going to shoot him. He closed his eyes. If he remained unconscious they wouldn't shoot him, he told himself. Not even the SS would execute an unconscious man. In the next moment, however, he realized they hadn't been fooled.

"He's coming to," one of them said.

"Bring some water."

He lay still praying for unconsciousness to take him back. But what should he do if it didn't? What should he do when they threw water in his face? Pretend? But they might see through it and jeer at him. Call him a coward. He didn't want them to jeer. He didn't want to be called a coward. He wanted to go with dignity.

"The nurse is here, Herr Hauptmann."

Hauptmann! The word exploded in his brain. That wasn't an SS rank. That was a Wehrmacht rank. A nurse!

Wehrmacht! Could it be, was it possible? He opened his eyes. The faces parted and a blonde woman entered his field of vision. She had a dark cloak thrown over her white uniform and wore a nurse's hat. Chase's heart leaped.

"Ciao Silvia," he rasped. His mouth was parched and his throat sore.

"Don't talk," she said, placing a hand on his forehead. She sat on the bunk, took hold of his wrist, and measured his pulse.

A soldier entered the cell with a canteen. He held it out to Silvia. "Acqua."

Silvia took the bottle, lifted Chase's head, and gave him to drink, little by little. Then she splashed some water on a cloth and proceeded to wipe his face.

"What is happening?" he asked her.

"You are being moved to the villa," she replied.

"Who are these soldiers?"

"Von Rota's men."

"Where are the Gestapo?"

"They are here. They are letting you go. Von Rota's men brought a release order." Silvia squeezed the cloth dry and replaced it in her medical bag. She looked up at the Hauptmann. "Barella," she said in Italian.

The other turned to the door. "Tragbahre," he called in German.

A soldier appeared with a stretcher. He unfolded it and they transferred Chase to it. Silvia wrapped a blanket round him and put a pillow under his head, and they left the cell, Silvia keeping by his side.

They made their way down the murky corridor smelling of disinfectant, the soldiers' hobnailed boots resounding on the stone. They climbed a flight of stairs and entered the front office. While the Hauptmann signed the release forms Chase observed the goings-on. The station was being fortified. SS men in combat gear were stacking sandbags by the window, a heavy machine gun was being set

137

up, magazines were being loaded with ammunition from boxes. From the noise on the ceiling similar activity was taking place on the upper floors.

The main door swung open and they left the building. The night was warm and damp, the street shining from rain. On the pavement stood soldiers with machine pistols at the ready. In the street were several vehicles: an ambulance, two gun cars, a radio car, and a low-slung armored troop carrier with gunports on the sides. The sound of gunfire and explosions was everywhere. At their appearance a lieutenant detached himself from the radio car and walked quickly to them.

"Herr Hauptmann, the partisans have set up barricades on Corso George Washington. We have to take a different route back."

"Take Corso Cavour," said the Hauptmann.

The soldiers lifted Chase into the ambulance and Silvia came with him. Engines revved, doors slammed, and the convoy moved off. It was dark inside the ambulance. Chase sought out Silvia's hand and drew her to him.

"What time is it?"

"Nearly two o'clock."

The ambulance swerved and both gun cars opened up on something with their mounted machine guns. Or maybe they were firing at nothing, thought Chase, simply spraying doorways. That was one of the new techniques for fighting in builtup areas: you blazed everywhere. Chase had read a paper on the subject prepared by the German Army based on their experience in the Warsaw uprising.

"What time did the uprising start?" asked Chase.

"Midnight."

The convoy picked up speed as they entered Corso Cavour, another wide boulevard lined with tall date palms. The roadway was deserted. From time to time, however, tongues of flame flashed from behind a tree or fence as a partisan franc tireur fired. Normally there was

138

never more than one flash because the shot was immediately answered by streams of multicolored lava from the gun cars.

"Can you stay the night with me?" asked Chase.

"Yes, I will. I will tell the hospital I have to bed-sit you."

"I don't want to be bed-sat. I want you in bed with me."

"I will bed-sit you *in* bed," she said, kissing him.

At that moment he couldn't think of anything he wanted more than to have her in bed by his side. Not for sex, since he wouldn't be able to perform even if he wanted to. Not for kisses, but for the sheer physical presence of a warm, soft body. The thought of waking up in the middle of the night alone petrified him. He was afraid he would have nightmares. With her by his side he would know that everything was over, that he was out of the clutches of Schumacher and his detectives. The very memory of that room made his flesh creep.

A convoy of fire trucks went by in the opposite direction, bells clanging to advertise they were noncombatants.

"Are there many fires?" he asked.

"Yes, many," she replied.

They held hands in silence, listening to the sound of the engine. As they passed through certain areas they could hear gunfire and explosions. In other areas nothing was happening. The fighting was checkered. On two occasions they were stopped by the Feldgendarmerie. Chase could hear the gendarmes tell the drivers to take detours because of fighting along the way. The instructions were accompanied by gay banter. Chase could tell the soldiers were enjoying the outbreak of fighting, a change from the monotony of garrison life. He envied them their gaiety, to be able to go into battle openly laughing. In this respect clandestine warfare was frustrating. It was silent warfare, nerve-wracking. Nor did you have the satisfaction of fighting to the finish with the enemy. It was mostly hit and run, which was to be expected, since stealth not bayonet charges were their métier. All the same, the constant lurking in the bushes got one down after a while. You started dreaming of one day being able to leap out of a trench, unsheath your sword and shout "Charge!" Then he remembered that soldiers in the trenches did not live in villas and didn't have girlfriends to fetch them from jail. When all was said and done, he decided, he would rather have things the way they were.

The convoy climbed a hill and turned into a driveway. The crunch of gravel told Chase they were home. The ambulance came to a halt, the doors opened, Chase was lifted out. On the steps under the front porch lamp stood the Boxers, weapons at the ready. The scene reminded Chase of some gangster movie with two gangs exchanging a body.

At the foot of the steps Romer and Kirilis took the stretcher from the Germans. "A second," Chase told them. He raised his voice. "Hauptmann." The other came up. "Thank you for getting me out of there."

"Our pleasure," the Hauptmann replied. He leaned close to Chase's ear and added, "The Wehrmacht looks after its friends."

The Boxers carried him inside with Silvia following. They took him upstairs to his room and deposited him on his bed. Romer went down to return the stretcher. The convoy drove off.

When Romer returned upstairs, both D'Arcy and Kirilis were standing outside. The door to Chase's room was closed. "What's going on?" Romer asked.

"Mrs. Chase is undressing Mr. Chase," said D'Arcy, lighting a cigarette.

They waited. Eventually the door opened. "Entrez messieurs." Silvia beckoned them.

They filed in, gathering round his bed. The chief lay in his pajamas, raised by pillows, grinning like a Cheshire cat. Men like to be babied and this one was unabashedly enjoying every minute of it.

140

Silvia said, "I'll be back in half an hour. I am going to the hospital to arrange to bed-sit Nick." She left the room.

The trio surveyed Chase the way people must have looked at Lazarus when he returned from the dead: awe mixed with curiosity. Rare was a man who came back from the basement of a Gestapo station.

"Want to touch me?" said Chase, breaking the spell.

"What did you get?" asked Romer.

"The gé-gène."

Kirilis let out a whistle.

"Congratulations," said D'Arcy.

"How many times?" asked Romer.

"Five."

Romer made a face that said he was impressed. "You must have balls of iron."

Chase grinned. "They feel like it now."

"Ice," said Romer. "Ice compresses. And tomorrow night have a woman on tap. You'll feel very randy."

Chase's eyes swept the group. "Whom do I have to thank for my release?"

"A communal effort," said Romer. "Szendroy traced you through his Carabinieri contacts, and we got in touch with von Rota."

"Von Rota told the Gestapo you were one of his men," said D'Arcy. "A G-2 officer."

"The Gestapo bought that?" said Chase.

"Didn't have much choice," said Romer. "Von Rota told them if they didn't release you, he'd send soldiers to get you."

"He also threatened to withdraw the soldiers he sent to guard them," added D'Arcy.

"How do you know all this?" asked Chase.

"From Silvia," said Romer. "Silvia's our go-between with von Rota."

"We did the ceasefire negotiations through her."

"Did?" Chase started.

"Yes, it's all arranged," said D'Arcy. "The ceasefire is

141

set for 0400. We talked to Depuis a few minutes ago. Rome took your advice and sent a liaison man. We've got a direct link with contact every hour."

"You mean *your* advice," said Chase. He pulled himself high on the pillows. "How's the uprising progressing?"

Romer answered, "The partisans have taken city hall and the police stations. The post office has changed hands twice. But the attacks on the barracks were apparently a failure. The rest is the usual confusion. Von Rota doesn't expect to have a clear picture until morning."

"Where is von Rota?"

"At the Kommandatur. He left the hospital an hour ago. He was only in for piles."

"We've also got a radio hookup with von Rota," said D'Arcy. "They gave us one of their radios."

"Has he countermanded the demolition order?" asked Chase.

"He's done one better," said D'Arcy. "He sent one of the SS companies to guard the Gestapo station, the other to strengthen the Kommandatur. There's no one to do the demolitions. At least for the moment. What's the program for after 0400?"

"If everything goes according to plan, the Germans bring back troops to quell the rising," said Chase. "And the partisans get massacred."

"Well, let's not have them massacred too much," said D'Arcy. "We don't want the Germans too strong. It might give them ideas. We don't want to be screwed twice."

"Jeff's right," said Romer. "We have to start playing poker."

By morning La Spezia presented a typical picture of a town on the first day of an uprising. Certain areas were in insurgents' hands, others in the hands of the occupant, while some were insurgent-controlled but contained enemy strongholds that made the control tenuous. Swastikas and the tricolors flew from opposite sides of a boulevard, sometimes even from the same side no more than two doors apart. In the insurgent areas there was a great deal of activity. Bedding and furniture tumbled from upper-storey windows to provide material for the building of new barricades and the strengthening of those already built. Loudspeakers blared songs and patriotic slogans. Soup kitchens dispensed food to red-kerchiefed warriors. In courtyards partisan action groups organized citizens' committees in the first step towards government. Civilian men were conscripted for military and labor duty. Patrols of Carabinieri gave way to patrols of men in suits with red armbands. In police stations the occupants of cells changed, the enemies of the previous regime being replaced by enemies of the new one. Everyone looked happy, some genuinely, some because not to do so could give rise to suspicion that the person had reactionary or bourgeois tendencies. By contrast, in the territory held by the occupant no one bothered about such things. The streets were deserted, the soldiers behind their walls of sandbags, the civilians in their homes behind closed doors and drawn blinds, both waiting. What they were waiting for appeared around ten o'clock from the direction of the port. They could even hear it before they saw it, the clang of tank threads followed by the darting figures of a Panzergrenadier battalion. The tanks rolled down Corso George Washington, plowing through the barricades. When they reached Via Mazzini, the force split in three. One continued straight, the other two turned north and south. Two hours later their task was complete. Von Rota had established the prerequisite to quelling any uprising, corridors constantly patrolled by tanks along which reinforcements could be moved to various parts of the city. The partisan commander, Piero-Piero, learned of this latest development while in the Boxers' sitting room waiting to be received by Chase, who was upstairs, held up by a radio transmission from Rome.

"There," said D'Arcy, handing him the decoded message.

Chase read the contents. "Very interesting," he said at the end. He put the message away. "Let's go."

They went downstairs, Chase supporting himself with a cane. He still felt weak although his testicles felt much better. In keeping with Romer's suggestion, Silvia had given him two ice compresses, one before going to sleep, the other upon waking up.

"Buon giorno Signori," said Chase, entering the sitting room. The others rose.

"This way please," said Romer, inviting them to the dining room.

They took seats, sitting on the same side they sat the last time, Piero-Piero, Bluter, the commissar, and Dario, the membership secretary, on one side, Chase and Romer on the other. But this time there were no pads or pencils for the partisans and the atmosphere was cold.

"What can we do for you, gentlemen?" asked Chase, opening the proceedings.

Bluter spoke up. "Last night," he began in a declamatory style that heralded a propaganda exercise, "the forces of the second partisan zone, in answer to repeated appeals from our American and English allies, launched an attack against the Nazi occupant and his Fascist lackies."

Wrong there, said Chase to himself. No one had asked them to stage uprisings. But to point that out would serve no purpose.

"Our valiant soldiers wrested from the Fascists the city hall, the police station, and many other strategic points, simultaneously occupying assault positions for the continuation of our offensive tonight. The objective of the uprising is to cut the enemy's supplies, demoralize him, and thereby hasten ultimate victory in our struggle against Fascism. This gallant gesture on the part of the partisans of Liguria is in danger of being nullified by unbelievable developments on the front. Four hours after the uprising

144

broke out, General Depuis, the commander of the 92nd Division, ordered a ceasefire. We demand an explanation."

"The reason is very simple," said Chase. "Our forces are low on ammunition and we have to conserve what we have in case the enemy launches a counterattack. It is my understanding that General Depuis' attack was premature. Rather than wait for his supplies to catch up, he decided to strike earlier, hoping to catch the enemy offguard or at least before he had fully reinforced himself. As it turned out, the enemy was firmly entrenched and the attack did not pierce the Gothic Line. A pause had to be ordered pending the arrival of supplies. General Depuis over-reached himself."

The Communist trio stared at Chase in a way that told him they were certain he was lying. By now the partisans were well aware of the fear with which the "Wind from the North" inspired the Anglo-Americans and their Italian capitalist allies. Nor would this be the first time they had been let down. At the beginning of the Italian campaign, as Allied troops were still down south, the Allied command called on the partisans to rise, promising seaborne landings along the coast all the way to Genoa, after which its troops would link up with the partisans. The partisans rose, the landings never took place, and the partisans were decimated. The Allied command attributed its decision to cancel the operation to the fortunes of war. The German coastal defenses turned out to be stronger than at first thought. The partisans attributed it to treachery.

"Is General Depuis aware that the Germans are withdrawing units from the Gothic Line to reinforce their garrison in La Spezia?" asked Piero-Piero. "We have information that an entire division—the 5th Mountain—is enroute by road to La Spezia. This morning landing craft unloaded tanks in the port. They were shipped up the coast from Massa near the Gothic Line. According to our information, the loading of those tanks began at two o'clock, two hours before the uprising even started. The

Germans were unusually well informed of Allied intentions."

"That's quite possible," said Chase. "The enemy can monitor our radio traffic with captured sets. But as regards the withdrawal of that division, I will most certainly inform General Depuis right away."

"Perhaps General Depuis could ask for air strikes against those troops," Dario threw in. "Or is the Allied Air Force also out of ammunition?"

"A very good suggestion," said Chase, ignoring the sarcasm. He turned to Romer, who was making a pretense of taking notes. "Mark that down, air strikes against the coastal road."

"The arrival of the tanks makes it essential that we be given bazookas and antitank artillery," said Piero-Piero. "We are also short of heavy machine guns."

"Mark that down," said Chase to Romer. "Bazookas, heavy machine guns, antitank guns."

Piero-Piero went on. "And if we are still to cooperate on Counter-scorch we will need more Stens with ammunition."

"More Stens and ammunition," said Chase to Romer.

"How soon can we receive a drop?" asked Bluter.

"That's difficult to say," said Chase. "It depends on the availability of aircraft, the requirements of other theatres of war. We should be able to receive a drop within a week, I think."

"A week?" Piero-Piero exploded. He turned to his partners. "Ma che commedia è questa?"

"It is not a comedy, Comandante," said Chase. "The war is not only being fought in Liguria. And the number of aircraft is limited."

"The last time you were able to get them within twenty-four hours," said Dario.

"For Counter-scorch we had booked aircraft well in advance," said Chase. It occurred to him that this might be as good a moment as any to express the Allied com-

146

mand's disappointment with the partisans' conduct on Counter-scorch, but he decided against it. In the circumstances it would be a bit hypocritical. What the partisans had done to the Boxers was no different from what the Boxers were doing to them now, taking them for a ride. The fact that it was the partisans who started the process was immaterial. If it had suited the Boxers to double-cross the partisans first, they wouldn't have thought twice.

"We must have those supplies within twenty-four hours," said Piero-Piero. "A week is too long. Against a reinforced garrison we will never last that long."

"Yes," said Chase, pensive all of a sudden. "If they bring back that division they could decimate you. Have you considered the possibility of negotiating a ceasefire?"

"A ceasefire?" exclaimed Piero-Piero. "Are you suggesting we abandon the uprising?"

"Not abandon it," said Chase. "Consolidate it. Would it not be wiser to consolidate your gains rather than lose everything? You hold what, a third of the town?"

"Almost a half," said Piero-Piero.

"Perhaps the Germans would be agreeable to let you keep it, provided you did not resume attacks against their half. And of course provided you allow them to resupply their strongholds in your areas so their men can eat."

"What makes you think the Germans would want a ceasefire?" asked Bluter.

"Because it would enable them to send that division back to the front. You must remember that the Americans could resume their offensive any day. A ceasefire in La Spezia would be as much to the Germans' advantage as to yours."

There was a long silence as the partisans considered this novel proposition. "No, we couldn't do that," said Piero-Piero finally. "The comrades wouldn't understand."

"It was just a suggestion," said Chase. "Very well, if there are no more points, perhaps we can terminate this meeting. I will message Rome and pass on your request. I will also message General Depuis. Where do we get in touch with you?"

"Our headquarters are in city hall," said Piero-Piero.

Dario opened his briefcase. "We have brought passes for you. They will enable you to get through our lines." He handed them to Chase. "I am sure you won't have problems getting through German lines."

Romer and Chase walked the partisans to their car. The villa was ringed with partisans armed with Variaras. They piled into two trucks and followed the delegation's car out the gate.

"Did you pick up that last remark from Dario?" asked Romer.

"Yes," said Chase.

"You think they know about our contacts with von Rota?"

"I wouldn't be surprised. They probably have party members among the nurses, too. We should warn Silvia and Francesca to be more discreet."

They went back into the villa. Romer collected his notes and burned them in the fireplace. They had no intention of messaging Rome with the partisans' request, but they didn't want the partisans to know this. In the circumstances it was preferable to blame everything on higher authority. If the partisans found out the Boxers were personally hostile to them, they might decide to pay them back with a rocket through the window. Irregular warfare was like that.

"Well?" said D'Arcy, joining them in the sitting room. "Did the partisans like your suggestion of a ceasefire?"

"Piero-Piero didn't," said Chase. "But I think what's his name, Bluter, might. I had the impression I gave him food for thought."

"In the end it will probably be he who decides if they go for it or not," said Romer. "According to Szendroy, in Liguria it's Bluter who is the real boss."

"How about von Rota?" asked D'Arcy. "Are you pitching him, too?"

"That's where Chris and I are going right now."

To get to the Kommandatur Chase and Romer had to cross a partisan-held area. They left their car at the barricade and continued on foot, Chase using his cane although as they progressed he seemed to need it less and less. A festival atmosphere reigned. Everywhere there were flags: hanging from balconies, flying from flag poles, strung between houses to form banners over streets. Most of them were tricolors of Italy but minus the Cross of Savoy, the emblem of the monarchy. That had been cut out and a piece of white sheet sewn in its place. Other flags were red: plain red, red with tricolors in the corner, red with a gold hammer and sickle. From loudspeakers attached to lampposts blared music: "Bandiera Rossa," the Internationale, the Marseillaise, "Avanti Partigiani," and other revolutionary songs, many of them in Russian. Between records came announcements: blood donors were needed by the Knights of Malta hospital, girls were wanted to serve as postmen, the Café Roma was serving free refreshments to partisans, a burned-out family sought two rooms. On corners, boys were shouting the headlines of Nostra Lotta, an insurgent newspaper just off the presses. The streets milled with people, office and shop workers taking advantage of the sudden holiday to promenade or engage in group discussions, partisans off duty sitting in cafés, and children everywhere, for they too had a sudden holiday from school. The partisans could be easily recognized by their paramilitary dress or the U.S. army fatigues and black berets that many of them had received from the drop the other day. In addition there were the red kerchiefs and the Stens. Every other man seemed to have a Sten, from the last drop and from previous drops whose contents were buried for this occa-

149

sion. In this particular area there was little fire damage but there were a lot of bullet marks on the walls. There was hardly any traffic, just the odd car or motorcycle with sidecar and some people on bicycles. That added to the festive atmosphere, and people walked in the middle of the streets.

"Was it like this in Warsaw?" asked Chase.

"Not nearly as colorful," replied Romer.

"There's nothing to beat a Mediterranean revolution for color and atmosphere," said Chase.

"I know," said Romer. "Everything looks better in the sun."

They passed a street where recruits to the partisan army were being trained in marching and keeping ranks and entered a square packed with people. In the center of the square was a raised platform. On one side sat a dozen or so women in two rows. They faced a woman in a chair whose hair was being shorn by a partisan. Another partisan was holding up a mirror so she could see herself. The woman kept avoiding the mirror with her eyes. A third partisan was addressing the crowd through a bullhorn, telling them the reason the woman was being punished. She had had an affair with a German soldier and had an illegitimate baby. The news was greeted with hoots, boos, and catcalls. Neither Chase nor Romer paid any attention to what went on on the platform as both found these head shavings disgusting. As far as they were concerned, if men don't want their women to sleep with the enemy they have but to fight harder to keep the enemy out of their country. Eyes straight ahead, Chase and Romer pushed their way through the crowd to reach the other side of the square to continue their journey. But a roar of laughter from the crowd made Chase turn and look up. He saw the woman in the chair trying to hit the partisan with the mirror. As his eyes swept the two rows who were awaiting their turn he stopped dead in his tracks. From this particular angle he could see all the women and one of them was the Gestapo woman inspector.

"What's wrong?" Romer asked, seeing Chase stop.

"The woman in the green blouse," said Chase in an undertone, "back row, second from the left. That's the woman I told you about this morning." Chase stared at the platform, a pensive expression on his face. An idea was forming in his head.

Romer waited, curious to see what would happen. That morning Chase had told him that before leaving La Spezia he would try to find the inspector and seduce her. It was one of those kinky fantasies men have from time to time, like sleeping with your teacher or seducing a nun. But what was interesting about Chase's fantasies was that he made them happen. Romer was curious to see how Chase would go about fulfilling this one. He suspected he would try to free the woman. But then what? That was the interesting part. It wasn't like Chase to say to a woman, "I saved your hair, now sleep with me." Nor was it his habit to go off on a tangent during a mission. Romer was sure Chase would come up with some scheme that would make her freedom an integral part of Counter-scorch. Chase used that trick all the time, getting a woman he liked to become a secret agent, then using this liaison to have a romance. This way no one could fault him. He could always say, "I had to sleep with her, it was vital to the mission." The astounding thing was that nine times out of ten these women did become vital to the success of the mission.

Chase beckoned Romer to follow him. He went up to a partisan and tapped him on the shoulder. "Partigiano, can you read?"

"Of course, why?" replied the partisan.

Chase handed him the pass from Dario. "Read this but don't say anything."

The other read it and returned it, clicking his heels in a silent "At your service."

"Who is in charge here?"

"The tenente."

"Take us to him."

The partisan led them through the shouting crowd to a requisitioned house outside which stood two partisans on guard. These had red stars freshly sewn on their berets. Inside was a large hallway. Behind a desk sat a sexy bambola in oversize U.S. army fatigues chewing gum that had been parachuted with the uniforms. Chase and Romer presented their passes and said they had to see the lieutenant on urgent business. The bambola motioned them to a room. They entered to find the place packed with the usual crowd of supplicants that materializes around those who have taken power. But they only waited ten minutes before someone came to fetch them. They were being given VIP treatment. They were led down a corridor and into the lieutenant's office.

"Capitano Romer!" the lieutenant behind the desk exclaimed. It was Nino's brother.

"Ciao Gianni," said Romer, shaking his hand. He introduced Chase, then went on. "What happened to you the other day? We even had vodka for you."

The other spread his arms in a gesture of helplessness. "Politics. What can one do? Believe me, Capitano, there isn't one man who doesn't regret it. Now if we are killed our families get nothing." He showed them to chairs. "How can I be of service to you?"

Romer looked at Chase, waiting for him to begin. The other said, "First we must tell you that there is an envelope waiting for you at the villa. Perhaps you could pick it up sometime. There is sixty thousand lire in it," Chase added, deciding in the circumstances to increase the sum, "which is our contribution to Nino's funeral. We would be grateful if you would pass it on to your parents. There will also be a medal, but that will come later."

"Sixty thousand lire!" exclaimed Gianni. "Capitano, you are most generous."

152

"Nino was a brave man," said Chase.

"What is the medal?" asked Gianni.

"We don't know yet. The decision rests with the Allied High Command. We simply describe the man's bravery and ask for a medal. The Allied High Command decides on what kind of medal. And now I would like to discuss with you a very important matter, but first I must request that you treat it as top secret. It is a matter that involves American security. Do we have your agreement?"

"If the subject is of such importance it will remain strictly between us."

"Thank you," said Chase. "We are looking for an agent of ours. A German woman. Our secret service had planted her in the Gestapo office in La Spezia. She worked there as an inspector. She is being held by your police and we need her."

"An agent of yours is being held by us?" asked Gianni incredulously.

"Her name is Gudrun Platz. In fact, we saw her just now. She's among the women on that platform in the square."

"A German woman on that platform? Those women are Italian. They're being punished for collaborating with the occupant. But let me check." Gianni rose and walked quickly to the door. "Corporal Asiago!" he shouted down the corridor. He returned to his desk. "Corporal Asiago should know, he's in charge of the head shavings."

"Si, Tenente?" A bookish youth in a civilian suit with an armband stood in the doorway. He had glasses with thick lenses.

"Those women having their heads shaved," said Gianni. "Is there a German woman among them?"

"Yes, Tenente, a woman who worked for the Gestapo."

"What is she doing having her head shaved?"

"The People's Court ruled she was not to be shot but was to have her head shaved in public. Tenente Maletti said to bring her to the square with the others."

"Bring her here immediately."

"Si, Tenente," said the other, closing the door.

"Your agent is fortunate," said Gianni. "All the Gestapo officials we catch are usually shot."

"She was in the administrative section," said Chase.

"Ah, that might be why the court was lenient."

"We will need a pass for her, similar to that Dario gave us," said Chase. "Can you make one out?"

"Yes, but its validity will be good only for this area," said Gianni. "If you need one for all areas, the pass will have to be signed by Comrade Dario."

"We'll get one like that later. For the moment one for this area will do fine. This way we can take her back with us."

Gianni opened a drawer and brought out a sheet of paper. He wrote out a pass, stamped it with two different rubber stamps, and signed it. "Ecco," he said, handing it to Chase. "I am glad I was able to be of service."

"If I may impose on you one last time," said Chase, "have you a spare office we could borrow for five or ten minutes? We would like to have a brief conference with her."

"Use mine. I have to meet someone downstairs. As a matter of fact, I am late," he said, looking at his pocket watch. "The medal for Nino, will it be an American medal?"

"Yes," said Chase.

"My father will be very proud."

"We will let you know as soon as we receive an answer from Rome. In the meantime, do you want to come to the villa for a meal and pick up the envelope or would you prefer we bring it to you? We could bring it tomorrow, perhaps."

"I would prefer you bring it. To get to you, I have to cross the German area and that is dangerous. For you, with your Argentinian passports, it is not so dangerous."

They said goodbye and he left. Romer looked at Chase.

154

The other tapped the wooden armrest of his chair in a touch-wood gesture. "Tonight," he said, "I want you to send a message to Rome requesting a medal for Nino."

The other nodded. After a while he said, "Wouldn't it be better for you to see this woman alone? My presence might inhibit her."

Chase pondered the suggestion. "Perhaps."

"I'd like to talk to some of the partisans," said Romer, rising. "I'll be in the vicinity." He left the room.

One look at her told him he would have to use a different approach. He had intended to be magnanimous, offer her freedom for her cooperation, but now it occurred to him she might turn him down. She had been beaten, there were bruises on her arms and two scratches on her face. Her clothes were rumpled and she looked dejected. She gave the impression of someone who is past caring. Nevertheless at the sight of him a spark of life appeared in her eyes. He could see she was happy to see him. All of which brought him to the conclusion that if she did cooperate it would be for him, not for freedom. To succeed he had to forget magnanimity, he had to talk her into it, charm her. They stood watching each other, she from the center of the room where the partisan had left her, he from by the window, cane in hand.

"Every time I see you you look so sad," he began.

"What is there to be gay about?"

"In my case I retained my testicles, in your case you will retain your hair. Isn't that a good enough reason?" A confused, puzzled expression crossed her face. "Yes, they gave me electricity." He hobbled up to her and scrutinized her cheek. "What did they do to you?"

"It doesn't matter," she said, looking down as if ashamed. He got the impression she was not ashamed at the way she looked but rather for having been a party to what had been done to him.

155

"Come, let's sit down," he said, taking her by the arm and leading her to a chair. She came willingly. "By the way, my first name is Nick. I am American." They sat down. "Are you hungry, do you want something to drink?"

"No thank you."

Chase's eyes swept her tussled hair, her grazed face, her rumpled clothes. "What happened to you?"

"After the uprising broke out I was arrested. Some partisans came to my apartment. I live near here. They wanted to know where the other Gestapo people lived. I told them there was no one in the area. They did not believe me and they beat me."

"Were there Gestapo officers in the area?"

"Yes. They found them anyway and they were shot. In the morning I was taken before a people's tribunal. I was told I was a war criminal. All Gestapo people apparently are war criminals. They were going to shoot me, too, but some women who lived on my street spoke up for me. I used to bring them medicines when their children were sick, sometimes food. The judge said that because I was a good German I wouldn't be shot. They would shave my head as punishment instead."

"They won't anymore. I've obtained your release."

"I am a prisoner of the Americans now?"

"No, you're free."

"Free? I don't understand."

"I told them you were an American agent. I even have a pass for you." Chase showed her the pass.

"I think I understand." She sighed, handing back the pass. "You want me to spy for you." By her reaction he could see she didn't like the idea.

"Yes."

"And if I refuse?"

"If you refuse," he said slowly, "I will be sorry we did not have a chance to work together. I would have liked that. But you will still be free. I will help you to go back

156

to the German-held area. We will say goodbye and never see each other again."

"Why are you doing this for me?"

He held her eyes for a moment. "Gudrun, are you so much of a Gestapo inspector that you can't guess?"

She went red as a beetroot and lowered her eyes. After a while she said, "Who will I have to spy on, my own, yes?"

"That depends on what you consider your own. What is your own? The Germany of Bach and Goethe and Frederick the Great? Or the Germany that murders women and children in gas ovens?" Once again he saw her face take on that puzzled, confused look. "Yes, my dear Frau, those rumors are true. Just like those rumors about electric torture machines are true. It's all true. The Führer might be a charming fellow, but what he has let loose is a reign of barbarism." For the next ten minutes Chase spoke to her of what was really going on in the occupied territories. He told her about the millions who were being exterminated in concentration camps. He cited names of people who had been exterminated, not Jews or Slavs or Gypsies, but Germans, Christian Germans, including priests and pastors. Then he told her—and this really got to her—of how the authorities brainwashed people like her to think these were merely rumors spread by enemies of the Reich so that to even voice them was unpatriotic. He compared this with the way her own people managed to hoodwink her. Even within the Gestapo only certain people knew of the tortures and for a good reason. The average German would be demoralized if he knew. For the average German to go on supporting the Nazi party he had to be made to believe the Nazis were normal people, that of course excesses did occur, but no more frequently than in any other country in the world. Then he told her about the Germans who had seen through the lies and the official mist, people like Rommel, heroes of Germany, who risked their life to stop the barbarism. "Today, Gudrun," he concluded, "there are two kinds of Germans. Those whose eyes have opened to the fact that the Nazi party was a mistake, and those who ostrichlike refuse to see it. To which do you belong?"

"I don't know." She sighed in frustration. "Everything is so complicated. It almost seems simpler to go back on that platform."

"Too late for that."

She gave him a long, silent stare. "What do you want me to do?"

"I want you to go back to your job and I want you to keep your ears open. I want you to let me know the moment the Gestapo decide to strike against the Wehrmacht."

"Strike against the Wehrmacht?" she asked, surprised. "The Gestapo?"

"For reasons I cannot disclose to you, there is this possibility, the SS and the Gestapo might decide to arrest the leading officers of the Wehrmacht in La Spezia. You will know about it because such things cannot be kept a secret within the organization itself. People will be assigned extra tasks to release others for the operation, cars will be arranged for, guards and drivers will be told they have to report at a certain time. Even if you don't know the exact nature of the operation, you will know something is up. I want to be informed. I will give you my telephone number."

"The telephones are cut."

"Only in partisan-held areas. The Germans cut them off here. In German-held areas they are working as usual. My number is three-three-nine-one. Can you remember that?"

"Three-three-nine-one, I'll remember it." Then her brow furrowed. "If I return to my job I will again be accused of being a war criminal. And this time they might shoot me."

"No, they won't. I'll make sure of that. Also, after we take La Spezia, you will be given the opportunity to work

158

for the American occupation administration. With your police experience and your languages you'll be very useful. Later you might want to work for the American occupation administration in Germany. But that is for later. For the moment your only problem is to get back to work. Tell them you escaped; that's the simplest. In an uprising, people escape all the time. Then you concentrate on tipping me off. The partisans and all that you forget about. I'll look after you. You must trust me."

"And you, are you prepared to trust me?"

He held her eyes. "Yes, Gudrun, I trust you." He could see that his words moved her, that it gave her pleasure to know he trusted her.

"I will work for you," she said.

"Excellent. Let's go."

On the way out Chase borrowed two partisans as guards. He and Romer didn't want to travel through the neighborhood alone with her. Someone might recognize her and start making trouble. They went to her apartment to pick up her most precious possessions, which Chase would take to the villa and keep for her. But the apartment had been emptied of everything: her jewelry, her clothes, even her furniture except for her bed in which lay a partisan and his girlfriend. On the doorknob hung a black scarf, probably the girl's. While her and her boyfriend's attention was diverted, Romer pocketed the scarf. Romer was a Catholic and knew that where they were going Gudrun would need a scarf, otherwise she would stick out like a sore thumb.

In the street they said goodbye to the partisans and headed for the German sector. En route they were stopped by a Fiat with police markings and a red flag flying. The occupants, civilians with armbands, asked for their papers. Seeing they were Americans they offered them a lift. Five minutes later, Chase, Romer, and Gudrun—wearing the scarf—were entering the Church of the Holy Cross. They went to the sacristy at the back and asked a nun polishing the floor for the priest. She went to fetch him.

"Good afternoon, Father," said Romer when the priest appeared. "I have a message from Gianni. He thanks you for saying the rosary for him."

"Come this way, please," said the priest. He led them into a room where two partisans were sitting. "These people are next," he told them.

The partisans led them to a small courtyard where there was a manhole. They lifted the cover, and one by one they descended a ladder into a sewer. When they were all down one of the partisans passed a rope, which they all took hold of. The partisans switched on their torches and the party began its eerie journey, the light playing on the slimy walls, footsteps resounding on the metal walk, surrounded by silence and dripping water. Rats scurried out of their way and bubbly noises came from the water below, sewer gas rising to the surface. In the distance they could hear a waterfall. The stench was suffocating at first but gradually they got used to it. Romer was reminded of Warsaw. It was there that the use of sewers as a means of communication originated. In the course of his stay in the city Romer had made many trips through the sewers. A Polish-speaker—Romer's father was a Polish mathematician who had emigrated to the U.S.A.—Romer had been sent to Warsaw during the rising to establish the feasibility of USAF drops to the insurgents. It was one of his least pleasant missions because while sentiment urged him to help the Poles he had to advise against such drops. For political reasons, however, Washington overruled his advice and one hundred flying fortresses made a supply drop in daylight. Romer was asked to report the results. Once again he had to give advice that went against the interests of the Poles—for even one container was a tremendous morale boost—that the drop was practically useless: nine-tenths of it fell in German-held areas. This time his advice was taken.

Romer had been relating his Warsaw experiences to Gianni while Chase spoke to Gudrun. During the conversation Romer had asked if the La Spezia partisans had heard about the usefulness of sewers. Which is when Gianni told him of the sewer route used to bring people out of the German-held area. Guessing that Chase would probably want to infiltrate Gudrun, Romer asked Gianni for a suitable route. That's when Gianni told him about the route that led from Holy Cross Church in the partisan zone to a courtyard of the Church of San Vito in the central German-held zone. And that's where they came out twenty minutes later. The partisans reentered the manhole for the return journey while the Boxers and Gudrun entered the church through the back door. There was no one about and they took a pew off to the side to clear their lungs and air their clothes. Then Romer told Gudrun where she had to cross the lines for the purpose of telling her story to the Gestapo. Finally Chase took her hand and squeezed it. "Schwein." In German the word pig meant good luck. With a nervous nod at both of them, Gudrun rose and walked out into the street.

"Nice woman," said Romer.

"I hope I am right about her," said Chase. "I'm playing this strictly by intuition."

"Best way," said Romer. "Always trust your intuition, old man."

When they got to the Kommandatur they found a message waiting for them from D'Arcy. He had sent it on the radio link between the Kommandatur and the villa. They were given it by von Rota's adjutant while waiting to see the general. The message passed on the latest instructions from Svenson in Rome. Knowing that Chase would not have the codebook on him, D'Arcy transcribed it into the Boxers' own code, one which they used for such occasions and which they all knew by heart. When he had

161

decoded the message, Chase passed it to Romer. The other read it, then reread the line, "Bear also in mind that arrival of mountain division could release SS sapper companies for scorching."

"This mission *is* turning into a poker game," said Romer.

"Isn't it?" said Chase. He could feel a headache coming on. Nerves.

The door opened and the adjutant bid them follow him. He led them into von Rota's office. The general was poring over the map table. At the sight of Chase's cane, his face clouded.

"What did they do to you?" he said, coming up.

"A little electricity, Herr General," Chase replied.

"The swines. I could shoot the lot of them."

"Herr General, may I present Captain Romer."

"Romer or Römer?" asked von Rota, shaking Romer's hand.

"Romer, the Polish branch." That one had ceased using the umlaut, the two dots over the *O*. Originally the family had come from Germany.

They sat down and, after enquiring about the general's piles without mentioning them by name, Chase stated their business. "Herr General, we have just received a message from General Clark. He asks that the La Spezia uprising be not turned into a massacre of the partisans."

"So he's not a Rokossovsky after all," said von Rota. "That will be the downfall of you Americans. You have a weak stomach."

"We're also a democracy, Herr General," Chase pointed out. "Rokossovsky's superior, Marshal Stalin, did not have to contend with a Polish vote. President Roosevelt has to worry about the Italian one. If the uprising in La Spezia ends in a bloody defeat for the partisans, the Communists will accuse the Americans of being responsible for it. Already they are spreading rumors that the halt in the offensive is purely political, that the Amer-

162

icans don't want the uprising to succeed because it is Communist. Such accusations could be exploited by the president's opponent in the coming election. It could lead to many Italian-Americans voting against Mister Roosevelt. The Italian electorate is an important one."

"Verdammt! Politics again." Von Rota reached for the cigarette box.

"The situation now is that although we still don't want to see the Communists win, we don't want them to lose either."

"That is typical politicians's logic," von Rota interjected, lighting a cigarette. "Continue."

"General Clark therefore proposes a moratorium, a ceasefire with both sides remaining in their present positions. He also proposes the return of the mountain division and the tank unit to their position on the Gothic Line. Communist propaganda is doing its best to link the division's withdrawal with the halt in the American offensive. The Communists are insinuating collusion. A return by the Fifth Mountain would belie these accusations. On the other hand, if the Fifth does not return, General Clark will be under ever increasing pressure to resume the offensive in order to prove there was no collusion."

"Aber das ist ein verfluchter Schwindel!" the general exclaimed angrily.

"On the contrary, Herr General, if it were a double-cross we would not be showing our cards. General Depuis would simply be ordered to break the ceasefire and punch his way through where the Gothic Line has been weakened by the Fifth's departure. I should point out that General Clark's proposal in no way alters our agreement of yesterday. Your safety and that of your family will be assured. On that you have my word of honor as an American officer. We are not preparing a one-sided moratorium. A ceasefire by you is conditional on a ceasefire by the partisans. If they refuse, General Clark will not resume his offensive until the rising has been quelled or

163

the partisans give up. But the partisans will not refuse a ceasefire. I am sure of that."

"Verdammt! I should have known this would happen." Von Rota fell silent while stroking his nose. He fixed Chase with a half-admiring stare. "You know, young man, you are a horse trader of the first order. Chapeau bas."

"Does that mean the general agrees to General Clark's proposition?"

"What else can I do?" exclaimed von Rota. "You have me by the throat in La Spezia, you have me by the balls on the Gothic." He resumed stroking his nose. "Well, at least von Palten will be pleased. He'll get his Fifth back. But what makes you think the partisans will accept a ceasefire?"

"A ceasefire would be to their advantage as well. If they don't agree, your mountain division will decimate them, especially since they lack sufficient heavy weapons."

"A propos, where are the weapons you sent them? We haven't seen them use any of those bazookas or artillery pieces."

"They didn't get them. I didn't know this, but the drop did not include heavy weapons. It was decided at the last moment to withhold them. I only found this out after our talk. Nor will they get them now."

"Have you been in contact with the partisans?"

"Yes, we have."

"Are they interested in a ceasefire?"

"They are."

"Who will be the intermediary?"

"My mission."

Von Rota fell silent in thought. "We will need access to our strongholds to bring food and evacuate sick personnel if need be," he said finally.

"That will be guaranteed."

"Very well. I will put a moratorium on all offensive operations immediately. The Fifth will be ordered to break camp where it is. I think it's three-quarters of the

164

way here. If the night passes without attacks from the partisans, I will order the Fifth back to von Palten in the morning and I will send back the tanks with the Panzergrenadier battalion. But if there is so much as one attack on any of our positions, the Fifth comes to La Spezia and the dynamiting of those factories begins first thing tomorrow. Is that clear?"

"It is clear, Herr General."

They got a lift to the German lines in a Kübelwagen. They used passes from von Rota to get through these. Then, holding white handkerchiefs over their heads, they walked through no man's land to the Italian barricade. For five hundred lire a man who owned a Harley-Davidson with a sidecar drove them to city hall, honking through crowds of promenading citizens. In this area, too, a festive atmosphere reigned, but there were more scars. Buildings were gutted by fire, many had window panes blown out, there were charred vehicles and potholes in the pavement from mortar bombs. The fighting had been heavy. At city hall they were told Piero-Piero was out but Bluter was in. Which suited Chase fine. For him Piero-Piero was too much the field commander, a brave fighter loved by his men, but not enough of the politician. Bluter on the other hand looked like a man who realized that at this stage of the war politics, not fighting, was the key to success.

"I have bad news for you," said Chase as they took seats in Bluter's office. "Our Air Force cannot give us planes for the next four days. They're booked solid."

"Peccato," replied the other simply.

"We passed on your request for air strikes."

"What did your people say?" asked Bluter.

"Nothing yet. That takes time, too," said Chase.

Bluter accepted the answer with a nod and said nothing.

"Where is that mountain division?" asked Chase.

"At last report the head of the column was in Lereto. About twenty kilometers from La Spezia. They'll begin arriving during the night. By morning the whole division will be here."

"You'll get massacred," said Chase.

"We'll get massacred," admitted the other.

Chase shook his head in feigned disbelief. "I don't understand. You must have a death wish. Surely the smart thing would be to agree to a ceasefire." He paused for greater effect. "At least until the drop can be made."

The other feigned nonchalance, but Chase could tell the last remark hit the mark. "You think the Germans will agree to a ceasefire?" Bluter asked.

"I told you already. They need one as much as you do. I just talked to our contact there. General von Rota is under pressure to return the Fifth to the front as soon as possible. The contact says if you will agree to a ceasefire they are prepared to halt hostilities right away. And the Fifth Mountain does an about-turn on the spot."

"How reliable is your contact?"

"He's never let us down."

"A ceasefire until the drop," Bluter mused pensively. "You think it would work?"

"I'm sure of it."

"Bene. We will suspend hostilities."

"Are you prepared to guarantee access to their strongholds?" asked Chase. "They have to be able to send food to their men. Also evacuate the sick or wounded."

"We are prepared to discuss that."

"So are they, but they want a guarantee in principle first. We have to vouch. Without a guarantee they won't go for a ceasefire. It makes sense."

Bluter nodded. "We guarantee."

"Now what about Counter-scorch?" asked Chase. "You still have to sign the agreement."

"We will sign when we get the drop."

Chase rose to go. "The order to suspend operations

must be received by all your outposts by nightfall. If there is so much as one attack, they will cancel the agreement. You realize that?"

"The order will be delivered to all sectors within the next hour. There will be no attacks."

"Goodbye, Commissario."

They went into the street. "Well done, Nick," said Romer, taking his arm.

The other shook himself clear, increasing his pace. As they passed the door of a burned-out building he darted inside and Romer heard him vomit. In all his time in the OSS Chase had never had to go through such nervous tension.

Chase came out, wiping his mouth. "Sorry about that."

"Come on, old man," said Romer, taking his arm again. "Let's go back to the villa and get drunk."

They didn't get drunk exactly, but they did have quite a bit to drink, so much so in fact that it was some time before either of them heard the telephone ringing. They had fallen asleep on sofas in the sitting room. The other two Boxers were upstairs, D'Arcy in the library taking down a transmission from Rome, Kirilis with Francesca in his bedroom. The Boxers had held another dinner party, but only Francesca could stay on afterwards. The other three had to go back to work. All the nurses at the hospital were having to work overtime because of the influx of wounded from the previous night's fighting.

"Pronto," said Romer, answering the telephone.

"Posso parlare a Nick?"

"Un momento per piacere." Romer cupped the receiver. "It's Gudrun."

Chase bounded off the sofa. "Si?"

"It's me," she went on in Italian. "How are you?"

"Not bad, and yourself?"

"Tired. I am on nights. One of your friends came by."

One of his friends, one of his friends. What could that mean? "Oh?" he said casually.

"A Mister something Grau."

Grau. Grey. Something grey. Something grau. Then he clicked. Feldgrau. Fieldgrey. The uniform of the Wehrmacht. Someone from the Wehrmacht had visited the Gestapo station. "What did he have to say?" he asked.

"Your visit seems to have upset him."

"I'm always upsetting people." He laughed.

"Anyway, what I am calling you for is to tell you that the dress you sent doesn't fit. It's too big. I'm sending it back. I've given it to some friends going your way. They'll drop it off. They should be there shortly. I hope you're up."

"I was going to bed, but I will wait for them. I'd better dress. Call you back." He slammed the phone. "Gestapo," he said to Romer. "They're coming here. Someone on von Rota's staff squealed." He bounded up the stairs. "Bolt the doors and douse the lights."

He ran to Kirilis' room. The door was locked. He rapped. "Frank."

"What do you want?" Kirilis replied from the inside.

"Get up. The Gestapo are on their way."

He ran into his room, loaded his Schmeisser, and slipped on his ammunition vest. On the way he collided with Romer.

"I think they're already here," said Romer. "I saw figures moving in the garden."

"Get the grenades. The case is in the bathroom cupboard, at the back under the towels. Put it on the landing. You and Frank take the downstairs, Jeff and I will stay upstairs."

He entered the library. D'Arcy was by the radio set, earphones on his head, taking down the transmission from Rome. On the table next to the set lay his Schmeisser and a torch. The radio was plugged into a car battery. Chase went up to him and brought his lips close to his right ear, the one he never covered with the earphone.

"The Gestapo are in the garden," said Chase in an undertone. The other nodded and went on writing down the columns of letters on the pad before him. "Von Rota has a Bulgar," Chase added. In OSS parlance Bulgar meant a traitor. "Can you cut?"

D'Arcy shook his head. "Category one," he said.

Category one? said Chase to himself. What could that be? They hadn't had one of those for a while. It meant a message of utmost importance.

The front door bell rang. Chase ignored it. He went to the table with the German radio set. He put the earphones on—like D'Arcy with one ear uncovered—turned the set on "send" and tapped out the call sign on the morse key. He switched to receive. There was no answer. He switched back to send and repeated the call sign. Downstairs the ringing gave way to pounding.

"Open up!" a voice shouted in German. "German police."

"Who is it?" Romer replied in Italian, pretending he didn't understand.

"Polizia tedesca," the man repeated.

"A moment. I will get the key."

In his earphones Chase heard the go-ahead. He sat down and tapped out a message in German. "Urgent. To duty officer. Inform General von Rota villa surrounded by Gestapo. Send relief. Youngman."

Downstairs the voice shouted, "Open up or we will break in!"

Chase waited for the Kommandatur to acknowledge receipt of his message then went to D'Arcy. "Can you use your torch?" he whispered.

The other nodded and turned the torch on.

Chase turned out the light and went to the window. Gently he parted the curtains. Below in the driveway stood a line of men with machine pistols. Chase replaced the curtain and left the library. The ground floor was in darkness, the only light now came from the corridor where Francesca stood leaning against the wall. She looked at Chase questioningly. Chase motioned her to stay put. The corridor was the safest place. The bedrooms had windows, and if there was a fire fight the Gestapo might lob tear grenades through them.

Downstairs shoulders were slamming against the front door. Chase ran into his bedroom and took a pillowcase off a pillow. He went to the landing and filled the pillowcase with grenades from the box on the landing. He climbed the ladder to the roof and opened the trapdoor. He laid out the grenades, then one by one he pulled the firing pin and lobbed them, two towards the front of the house, two to the back and two to each side. The explosions were followed by screams and shouts. When he returned to the landing, the pounding on the door had ceased.

D'Arcy came out of the library. "What were those explosions?" He had finished.

"I was throwing grenades. If we can delay their attack long enough, von Rota's men might get here in time."

"Did you call him?"

"I sent a message on the hookup."

"I'd call him as well," said D'Arcy. "For all we know the Bulgar might be an adjutant or a radio operator. Von Rota might never get the message."

"That's a thought," said Chase. "Okay, I'll call him."

"What do you want me to do?" asked D'Arcy.

"Decode that message. If it really gets bad, I'll call you."

Chase tiptoed down the stairs. He took the telephone off the hallway table and lay on the floor. He was about to lift the receiver when the telephone rang. "Si?" he answered.

"It's me again. The ceremony you were asking about is for midnight." She hung up.

There was the sound of breaking glass from the kitchen and a burst of gunfire rent the inside of the house. A man screamed in pain, and everything fell silent again.

"What was that?" asked Romer in a loud whisper.

"A guy was trying to get through the kitchen window," said Kirilis.

Chase dialed the Kommandatur. "This is Hauptmann Jung. Give me General von Rota. Hurry."

"Von Rota." In the background laughter could be heard. A party.

"Herr General, this is Captain Chase."

"Herr Chase," said von Rota gaily. "How nice to hear from you. What surprises are you going to unveil for me now? New propositions from . . ."

The words were lost as Romer's Schmeisser fired in the direction of the sitting room windows. This time the Gestapo replied. Tracer bullets flew into the house, breaking glass, churning plaster, overturning lamps, the colored projectiles ricocheting off the walls, the air filled with dust.

"Herr General!" Chase shouted into the mouthpiece, "the Gestapo are going to attack you at midnight. They will try to arrest you and your staff. You have a traitor. He told the Gestapo about our meetings. What? I can't hear you. Yes, the Gestapo are here. They are shooting at us, they have surrounded the villa. I sent you a message on the radio. Yes, we need help. Quickly. Yes, we'll try." He hung up.

"Throw more grenades!" Romer shouted as the bullets continued thudding into the walls.

Chase bounded upstairs. He filled the pillowcase again and climbed to the roof. Another eight grenades flew in all directions. He didn't throw any more because he had to conserve them. They only had one box. This time from the driveway and the garden tracer bullets rose in reply, but they flew harmlessly overhead. From that angle it was impossible for the men downstairs to hit him. He descended the ladder back into the corridor.

"Nick, will we be all right?" asked Francesca, pale with fright.

"Don't worry, everything will be fine," he said, hurrying past her into the library.

By the window stood D'Arcy with his weapon. "You got at least two of them." He poked his machine pistol out of the window and let off a burst. He stood back, expecting a reply.

Instead a bullhorn blared below: "Feuer einstellen! Feuer einstellen!"

The gunfire ceased.

"You in the house," the bullhorn continued, "you have ten minutes in which to leave with your hands up. If you don't, we will come after you with gas. Ten minutes."

"I wonder why ten?" said Chase, peering down from another window.

"No doubt that's how long they figure it will take for the grenades to arrive," said D'Arcy. "I bet they radioed for them the moment we started shooting."

Chase walked out of the library onto the landing. "Chris, Frank, are you okay?"

"We're fine," said Romer.

"When is the Wehrmacht cavalry coming?" said Kirilis.

"The general said he would send men right away."

"You see, he's a gentleman," said Francesca. "Didn't I tell you?"

"You're quite right, Francesca," said Chase. "Meanwhile, why don't you come and sit down in the library. You've been standing long enough. This might take a while yet."

In fact, it ended sooner than any of them expected. A Puma roared up the driveway, a searchlight swept the grounds, and a loudspeaker blared: "By order of General von Rota, military governor of La Spezia, all Gestapo personnel are forthwith confined to their quarters. Return to your cars. On your way out, at the gate, you will be asked to surrender your weapons. Do not resist, do not take evasive action. The villa is surrounded."

One by one the Gestapo agents emerged from the bushes. Some tried to start an argument with the car commander but he wouldn't have any of it. Cursing him, they walked down the driveway to the street. At the gate soldiers took their weapons. The agents got into their cars and drove away. The Wehrmacht soldiers remained.

"Are you going to guard us?" Chase asked the commander of the armored car.

"We're waiting for the general," he replied. "He's supposed to come here."

A short while later an open Mercedes-Benz command car with swaying antennas swept up the driveway accompanied by two gun cars. The escort jumped out, the door opened, and von Rota stepped out.

"I must say, Captain Chase," said von Rota, "you certainly keep your word. When you said you would assure my safety I never imagined it would be from my own. Those swines in the Gestapo had organized a mutiny. They were going to use the SS company stationed at the Kommandatur to arrest me. Thanks to you, we beat them to it." Von Rota turned to a man in the command car. "Hans, pass the Schnapps." He took the bottle. "I thought we might celebrate together our good fortune."

They went to the villa. Von Rota sniffed the air. "I smell a familiar perfume."

"Gunpowder, Herr General," said Chase.

"No, no, a woman's perfume."

"Hello, General," said Francesca, appearing on the landing.

"What did I tell you? Signorina Francesca, how nice to see you. Are you part of the garrison or another relief force?"

"Signorina Francesca manned our medical services during the seige," said Chase. He led the general up to the library, the sitting room being in a mess. He presented

173

D'Arcy and Kirilis. "The last two members of the mission. Now you have met everyone. Frank, bring some glasses," he said to Kirilis in French.

Von Rota threw a glance at the books lining the wall. Speaking French, he said, "I envy you your library. Did you bring it with you?"

"The general must be joking," said Chase.

"I thought you might have." Von Rota smiled. "After all, you people do have a reputation for fighting wars surrounded by all the comforts of home."

"Russians say the same things about the German Army," countered Chase.

"I grant you a point," said von Rota, inspecting titles. "I suppose comfort, like everything else, is relative." The SSTR caught his eye. "Ah, a bandit radio transmitter. I must see this." He walked over. "How interesting, so small."

D'Arcy explained the set, told him about the playbacks and electricity games. Then the glasses arrived. They drank a toast to their fortune and Romer passed a plate of hors d'oeuvre left over from dinner to chase the Schnapps. There followed some chit-chat about clandestine warfare and another round of drinks, after which Chase nodded to the others to leave him and the general alone. When the others had left, he said, "We have received another message from General Clark."

"Another proposition?" said von Rota.

"Yes."

Von Rota reached for his silver cigarette case. "General Clark is beginning to remind me of one of those magicians with a hat. After one rabbit there's another rabbit. What is he proposing this time?"

"Is the General familiar with Operation Sunrise?"

"No, I am not," said von Rota, lighting his cigarette. He stuck the cigarette in his holder and settled back. "What is it?"

Chase told him.

A day earlier secret surrender negotiations had opened in Switzerland between the Allies and the German military command in northern Italy. What prompted the Allies to undertake them was the Communist activity in northern Italy. After La Spezia, uprisings had broken out in Bologna, Parma, Reggio, and Modena. Risings were also being prepared for Genoa, Turin, Milan, and Venice. All over the north the Communists were rising for the kill, and it was becoming apparent that the Allies would be arriving to find towns in Communist hands, with the Italian political opposition wiped out so there would be no one to contest the postwar elections. For political reasons the Allies could not repeat what they did on the Ligurian part of the Gothic Line. Along the rest of Italy the offensive had to continue, to the detriment of their interests, political as well as economic. Ravenna was a good illustration of the latter. A rising broke out a few hours after the one in La Spezia. Prepared for it by events in La Spezia, the military governor in Ravenna ordered scorching to begin. By morning the city's factories were in ruins. There were no other OSS Counter-scorch teams in the north, only La Spezia had one. Which created another complication. In New York, an official of Kramer while listening to a friend moan of his investment losses in Ravenna boasted of his company's coup in getting the OSS to protect Kramer industry in La Spezia. A chance remark, but it spread like wildfire. In Washington, the Capitol's switchboard lit up with calls from people on Wall Street demanding from congressmen the same protection for *their* investments in Italy. The pressure was on to end the campaign quickly. Feelers were put out to the Germans. As it happened they, too, were interested to end the fighting, though for different reasons. In the case of the Germans the reason was personal safety; the partisans had followed their capture of Ravenna with a bloodbath. The jails were opened and victims of German mistreatment went on a rampage of revenge. Following

175

the example of Naples, the military governor and his wife ended up on meat hooks, other officers were hung from lampposts regardless of whether they were Wehrmacht or SS. An end to the war would free Allied troops for immediate dispatch by air to major northern towns where they would take power directly from the Germans, thus avoiding a Communist interregnum. The safety of German officers and their families would be assured. After explaining this, Chase went on:

"A signing is expected within two or three days. But in the meantime there is La Spezia. The pressure is increasing for General Clark to resume the offensive on the Ligurian sector. As feared, the halt in the offensive has been raised by the president's opponent in a speech to an Italian-American organization. The papers have picked it up and we can be certain the Communists will do their best to blow it out of proportion. In view of this General Clark asks whether you, General von Rota, would be prepared to turn the ceasefire into a surrender. A surrender is coming anyway. You would be making yours a few days earlier, that's all. The matter has been raised with General Halbestramm, who has informed us he would not object, provided of course you agree. By agreeing you will be extricating General Clark from an embarrassing situation. An agreement by you would be considered by General Clark as a personal favor. In return he offers to make your captivity a pleasant one. You and your family—and that includes your son—will be alloted a villa in Capri for the duration of hostilities. Upon Germany's surrender you will be flown to your country and provided with suitable quarters pending the recovery of your estate in East Prussia. Furthermore General Clark authorizes me to state that you will be given immunity from any court action that might arise as a result of those reprisals you took against the partisans for the grenade attack on the club. The immunity will cover

176

all court actions whether from individuals or the Italian state. General Clark invites you to answer his proposal by morning."

The other stroked his nose in silence. A very long silence. "I will have to check this with General Halbestramm," he said finally. "I will also have to discuss it with my staff." Von Rota rose. "You will have my answer by eight o'clock."

The minutes ticked by. Ten to eight. Chase paced the sitting room impatiently. From the hotel garden came the sound of mandolins, the orchestra practicing again. Nine to eight. Will he or won't he? Everything pointed to von Rota saying yes. That was the trouble. From experience Chase knew that when everything said black, that's when chance came out with white. It had happened time and time again in the past. The last time in Belgium. They had gone to get a Jewish scientist out. They found him, talked to him, convinced him. The Lysanders were on their way. Everything was go. And then the guy decided he didn't want to leave his homeland after all. At the last moment someone convinced him he wasn't really in such danger. The Nazis wouldn't harm him, he was too important. The Boxers flew away emptyhanded. The same could happen on this job. Logic dictated von Rota would go for a surrender. But all it would take to upset logic would be a chance remark from his son. For instance, "I thought, Papa, you said a von Rota never surrenders." Or words to that effect, and bingo, the whole thing would somersault. What if it did somersault? What if von Rota said no? Chase asked himself for the nth time. And for the nth time he dismissed the thought. The implications were too depressing to consider. Chase was longing to wind up this mission. He had had enough of Counterscorch. He was tired of the constant running back and forth with those, "If they do that, will you do this," tired of the bluffing, the lying, the nerves, the tension, tired of playing poker, as Romer called it. To think he didn't even know which was worth more, a full house or a flush. That's how much he knew about poker; the only card game he played was bridge. Chase glanced at the man fixing the shot-up windows. The man was humming, happy, cheerful. A carpenter, said Chase to himself, that's what he should become. Work with your hands. No intrigues, no bluffing, no nerves, no vomitting from nerves. A good, healthy life . . .

"Rrrrring! Rrrrring!"

"Yes?"

"Good morning Captain Chase. Von Rota here."

"Good morning, Herr General." On the landing upstairs figures appeared. Romer and D'Arcy. "Did you sleep well?" Chase asked.

"I haven't slept since I left you," von Rota replied. "Regarding the proposition we discussed . . . No, not that file, the other one. The one with the blue cover. Sorry, that was my new adjutant. I have a new adjutant to replace my Judas. It was my old adjutant who reported our talks to the Gestapo."

Get on with it! Chase felt like shouting. A third figure appeared on the landing. Kirilis.

"Regarding the proposition. Yes, I am ready to accept."

Chase's hand shot out in a thumbs-up sign. "I am very pleased to hear that, Herr General. I shall communicate your decision immediately. Then, perhaps, we could discuss its implementation. When would be a convenient time to do this?"

"Anytime. I'll be in the Kommandatur all morning. The sooner the better."

Chase put the receiver down. He smacked his fist against his palm. "We did it." He looked up at the others and shouted. "We did it!"

"Die Fahne hoch," intoned Romer.

"Die reihen fest geschlossen," the others picked up, treating themselves and the carpenter to a rousing rendition of the Horst Wessel song.

The scene was a glittering one, Wehrmacht officers resplendent in evening dress uniforms, women in gowns swirling with perfume, the orchestra playing operetta music, white-gloved waiters pouring champagne, the whole thing lit by chandeliers. The occasion was a reception for the American ceasefire commission given by von Rota in the dining hall of the Kommandatur. The commission, twenty-odd officers, had arrived earlier in the day to make arrangements for the laying down of arms on the morrow.

"American uniforms are somewhat staid compared to German ones, don't you think?" said Gudrun.

Chase laughed. "Compared to German uniforms everything is staid. You have the smartest uniforms of any army."

"I'll have to give up my black uniform for a khaki," said Gudrun. "A pity. My black one was much better cut."

"But the money will more than make up for the cut of the uniform, I am sure," said Chase.

"Very true. I will be earning twice what I made in the Gestapo."

"Bonsoir." It was D'Arcy, looking very Germanic all of a sudden, perhaps because the black of his dinner jacket brought out his sandy hair. All the Boxers were in dinner jackets. Chase had ordered them up from Rome, where they had left them prior to coming to La Spezia. They were flown over by Svenson's private Mosquito. In the OSS, that sort of thing was normal. The transport was there and gentlemen, especially OSS gentlemen, did not attend gala receptions in lounge suits.

Chase introduced D'Arcy to Gudrun. "Madame is joining our military police," he explained.

"A welcome addition," said D'Arcy, giving her an admiring glance. In her Gestapo dress uniform, a well-cut black gown, she looked very attractive.

"What is that saying?" said Chase. "Armies come and go, but the police remain."

"As does the taxman," added D'Arcy.

"Good evening."

"Frau Platz, permit me to present the fourth member of our unit," said Chase. "Captain Kirilis."

"Enchanté, Madame." Kirilis bowed, his pencil mustache freshly trimmed. He glanced round the room. "I have to say this is a most original way of beginning a surrender."

"When you're a Junker with a millennium of victories and defeats behind you, you try to enjoy both, I suppose," said Chase. "Where is Chris?"

"I saw him a while ago consoling Szendroy," said Kirilis. "The partisans made him burn an entire art exhibit. Pictures by a fascist painter. Szendroy says he lost a hundred thousand lire in art."

"That must be the exhibition we saw, the night you were . . ." D'Arcy let the words trail, realizing he was about to commit a faux pas.

"I talked to General Depuis on the radio just now," said Kirilis. "Our sappers will be here at 0600. We're to rendezvous with them by Pier Six for a briefing on what has to be de-mined."

"You can look after that," said Chase. He turned to Gudrun. "Captain Kirilis is our demolition expert. He loves blowing things up. For him Counter-scorch has been a most frustrating mission."

"Where did you get that idea?" said Kirilis. "Counter-scorch has been a most delightful mission."

Chase looked at him, puzzled, then remembered Francesca. "Yes, of course, I forgot." He laughed and said to

Gudrun, "Captain Kirilis was wounded in a skirmish a few days ago. He found himself a ravishing Italian red-head to nurse him."

"And you?" asked Gudrun with a playful smile. "Have you found a ravishing redhead?"

"No, I came across a ravishing brunette in a certain police office."

Suddenly the music stopped. "Ladies and Gentlemen," said von Rota's adjutant, climbing onto the platform, "I have a brief announcement to make. Would all officers quartered in the Kommandatur please rejoin their units. Thank you." The music resumed.

"What was that, I wonder?" said Kirilis.

"I don't know," said Chase, "but one of us better find out. Excuse me."

Chase followed the officers out of the door. In the corridor he was passed by running soldiers putting on helmets and strapping on combat gear. As he passed an open window he heard gunfire. Diable! he swore to himself. New complications. He entered the command post. The place was humming. Half a dozen radio sets were going at once, telephones rang nonstop.

"Captain Chase." Von Rota waved him over. "Your partisan friends have broken the ceasefire. They're attacking administrative targets all over the city. The post office and the water works are already in their hands. It looks as though they used the ceasefire as a cover to infiltrate more men. I am afraid this may turn into a very unpleasant caper. We have hardly any troops."

"What about your tanks, Herr General?" asked Chase.

"Young man, thanks to you those tanks and that Panzergranadier battalion are now sailing down the coast to the Gothic Line."

"And the Seventeenth?"

"Confined to barracks at the request of Colonel Burke (head of the ceasefire commission). He wished to avoid

181

provoking the partisans." The general snorted. "As if the partisans needed provoking."

"And the sapper battalion?"

"The two SS companies I disarmed last night, and of the other three, one is at the dam, another at the port, and the third here. Bref, my dear Captain, we have a little over a hundred men to defend us. Neither of the other two companies will be able to reach us in time. To get here they would have to cross the partisan zones. The Luftwaffe half-battalion is hors de combat, also confined to barracks at the request of Colonel Burke."

"Can't you get them out of barracks?"

"Not when the barracks are surrounded by several thousand partisans. The same applies to the Seventeenth. No, I'm afraid it looks as if we're in for a miniature Stalingrad."

"Permission to use a telephone, Herr General."

"Help yourself."

Chase grabbed a telephone. "Get me three-three-nine-one," he told the switchboard operator. "Quick."

"OSS, Sergeant Mitko speaking." The villa now had a duty sergeant.

"Captain Chase here. Where's the Ninety-second?"

"Last I heard they were bedding down for the night in Lereto. They took the surrender of the mountain division."

"I want a message sent to General Depuis. Top priority." Chase dictated the message. "Send it off right away. Another thing. Hello? Hello?" Chase slammed the phone down.

Behind him he heard a voice say, "Alfa reports bandits in control of the telephone exchange."

A telephone rang. An officer picked it up. "Yes? Yes. Right." He put the phone down. "All the lines are down, civilian and military. We have no telephone communication."

"They probably cut us off at the exchange," said someone.

The door opened and a young lieutenant entered, his face flushed. "Herr General," he saluted, "bandits are attacking the Kommandatur." Just then the windows rattled.

"Sir?" a radio operator said to Chase. "Someone wishes to speak to you on the radio-telephone."

"Who is it?" said Chase, following him to the set.

"I don't know."

Chase took the receiver. "Captain Chase. Over."

"This is Major von Rota. I am at the dam. I am holding you personally responsible for my father's safety. It's you who got us into this mess. If my father is taken by the partisans the dam goes up. You know what that means? Over."

"I know what it means and I don't like your tone or your threats. Your father's safety is as much my concern as yours. American troops are on their way and will be here shortly. In the meantime I suggest that you direct your energy to trying to break through the partisan-held area and help us defend the Kommandatur. Over."

"Captain, I am not interested in any more of your suggestions or your proposals. We're tired of listening to them. Simply remember what I told you. If my father is taken, I flood the town. After that, if there's anything left, I'll start dynamiting. I'll turn La Spezia into another Warsaw. Over and out."

A loud explosion rattled the windows. A field telephone rang. A voice in the room called out, "E Company reports bandits have dynamited the front gate and are attacking the courtyard."

"Sir?" the same radio operator said. "You are wanted on the villa hookup."

Chase went to the transmitter. He sat down and tapped out on the morse key. "Boxer here, go ahead."

The other messaged, "From General Depuis. Armored cars en route from Lereto. Division following. FYI our telephone line down. Mitko."

Chase tapped back, "FYI partisans have cut lines." He signed off.

Another explosion rattled the windows. Chase looked about for von Rota but he had left. The adjutant was around, however. "Herr Major," he said, going over to him. "Can you lend me a bullhorn?"

"You mean a loudspeaker? We might have some in the storeroom. What do you need one for?"

"Tell you on the way."

They went out of the command post. In the corridor, members of the orchestra and civilian guests were making their way to the back of the building away from the fighting. They were hurrying, but there was no panic. From somewhere downstairs came the hammer of a Spandau firing.

"Nick!" It was Kirilis. "Where have you been?"

Chase told him. "Where are the others?"

"In the back of the building. With the ceasefire commission. Gudrun is with us."

"Explain the situation to Burke," said Chase. "I'll join you later."

In the storeroom there was a whole row of bullhorns. He chose one, put in a fresh battery, and they went back to the command room. The general was back, poring over a map. Chase told him of his plan.

"You're wasting your time," he replied. "On top of which you might get shot."

"I'd like to try."

"Very well. Come."

They walked along several corridors until they came to rooms overlooking the courtyard. They entered one with French windows that gave onto a balcony. Below, tracer bullets flew back and forth as the attackers fought it out with the defenders. Chase opened the doors and the noise of battle filled the room. He put the bullhorn to his mouth.

"Cessate fuoco! Feuer einstellen!" He advanced two

184

paces towards the balcony. "Cessate fuoco! Feuer einstellen." Gradually the firing died down.

Chase stepped onto the balcony. "Partisans! This is Captain Chase of the American Army speaking. I have a message from the Allied High Command. To the partisans of La Spezia. Victory is ours. A few minutes ago the German commander of La Spezia signed an agreement of surrender. American troops are on their way to take over. They will be here in an hour. The war in La Spezia is over. Partisans! Do not jeopardize the agreement. Withdraw from the German zone and await the arrival of the Americans. Victory is ours. Long live the partisans of La Spezia. Long live the Volunteers of Liberty. Long live Marshal Stalin. Long live President Roosevelt. Long live—" He broke off as a stream of tracers rose towards him. In the next instant everybody opened up on everybody. The battle was on once again.

"No good!" Chase shouted running back in.

"What did I tell you?" said the general.

They hurried to the command post.

"There he is," said Kirilis from the doorway of a small office adjoining the command room as Chase entered.

Chase went over. At a radio D'Arcy was fiddling with knobs while at a table Romer was studying a map. "What's up?" said Chase.

"Depuis has asked for a breakdown of the city by sectors," explained Kirilis.

"Ready?" said Romer.

"Anytime," said D'Arcy, reaching for the morse key.

"Partisans sector Lima Bravo eight four nine three zero," Romer dictated. "German sector Lima Bravo seven . . ."

"We're sending it to the villa," said Kirilis. "Mitko is on passing."

A field telephone rang in the command room. An officer answered it. He cupped the receiver. "Herr General, E company say they can't hold much longer."

"Tell them to hold as long as they can," said von Rota.

Chase and Kirilis went up to him. "What's the situation?" asked Chase.

"E company is taking heavy casualties. They're too exposed. On the other hand, if I pull them back the partisans will be able to reach the front doors. Then we'll have a battle between floors."

"If they get a foot inside, they'll swamp us," said a colonel, the general's chief of staff.

Von Rota turned to Chase. "How long before the Americans come?"

"They should be here within the hour," said Chase.

Von Rota surveyed the plan of the building, spread out on the table before him. "The only way they can get into the building is by the front door," he mused aloud. He circled an area of the map with his hand. "If we could bring this part of the building down we could block the entrance with rubble. Then we could sit tight and await the Americans."

A loud explosion shook the building. The field telephone rang. "Herr General," said the officer, "bandits have dynamited the front door. E Company is retreating to the first floor."

"So much for blocking the entrance," said von Rota. "We should have thought of that earlier."

"Explain the situation to me," said Kirilis to Chase. He did not speak German.

Chase told him what was happening. "Now that the partisans control the foyer we can't block the entrance. It's too late."

"Not necessarily," said Kirilis. "Vous permettez?" he said to the general, going round to his side of the table. He leaned to study the plan of the building, then said, "Why don't we try the following?" He told them what he proposed.

A few minutes later Chase entered the room where the ceasefire commission and civilians were sheltering from

186

the fighting. "We need volunteers as porters." They all volunteered. He told the men to follow him. He led them to a room on the third floor. The shelves were stacked with explosives. There were blocks of nipolit, sacks of Sprengmunition 02, metal containers filled with ammon saltpeter, boxes of pikrinsaure, and plastite.

"Everyone grab something to carry and form a column outside!" shouted Kirilis. He helped himself to detonators and a hand blasting machine, and harnessed a roll of firing wire on his back. "I guess I'll get my bang out of Counter-scorch yet," he said to Chase.

The column set off upstairs to the fourth floor then moved along corridors to the front part of the building. They arrived at an elevator shaft. As the electricity was out in that part of the building, Romer and D'Arcy were cranking it up by candlelight. When it arrived Kirilis pried the door open and they loaded the elevator with the explosives. Then Kirilis inserted detonators attached to a firing wire.

"Wind it down," Kirilis ordered, passing out the wire. He turned to Chase. "When that baby goes off several hundred of those partigianos will go with it. That'll teach them to double cross honest citizens like us." He grinned.

The cranking mechanisms squeaked, the elevator descended. From below, through the shaft, came the sound of battle: men shouting, grenades exploding, the rattle of machine guns.

"Nick, take over!" shouted D'Arcy.

Chase took over and D'Arcy borrowed a torch from the general. He shone into the shaft. Soon he could see the counterweight. When it rose to halfway between the third and fourth floor, D'Arcy shouted to Romer to stop. This meant the elevator was now halfway between the ground floor and the basement.

"Everyone clear out!" shouted Chase.

They all ran to the back of the building, the ceasefire commission to their room, the Boxers with the general to the command room, Kirilis passing out wire all the time. In the command room the general called E company and told them to evacuate the front of the building. Kirilis attached the detonating wires to the hand blasting machine.

The field telephone rang. "Front part evacuated," an officer announced.

Kirilis made the sign of the cross and took the handle of the blasting machine.

The wall opposite the window flashed green.

"Hold it," said Romer. He walked quickly to the window and opened it.

Green flares were exploding in the sky, and over the gunfire a loudspeaker was blaring, "Cessate fuoco! Cessate fuoco!" The accent was American.

"Lucky Commies," said Kirilis, putting aside the blasting machine.

To the strains of the march from *Aida,* played by the La Spezia fire department band, the Boxers climbed the steps of city hall to receive their medals. A festive atmosphere reigned in the square. The balconies were draped with red-white-green flags once again bearing the cross of the monarchy, Carabinieri held back the crowds, and city officials fresh out of jail beamed good will. A public holiday had been declared to celebrate victory. Victory over whom? The mayor's proclamation did not specify. Nor did anyone specify in the speeches that preceded the award of medals. The Boxers reached the top of the steps and came to a halt. A small man in a red sash, flown from Rome by the Italian government, came up to them followed by a Carabinieri with a scarlet pillow. On the pillow lay four medals, the Cross of Savoy. One by one the man pinned them on the Boxers, shook hands, then returned to his spot. The band played the American and Italian anthems; the ceremony was over. As the Boxers descended the steps, a black limousine pulled up. Flash-bulbs popped and the heroes of La Spezia—that's how the mayor described them—drove off, heading for the port. Jeeploads of black faces passed them. The 92nd was a black division.

"We're an hour late," said Chase, glancing at his watch.

"Aren't we saying goodbye to the nurses?" asked D'Arcy.

"They're meeting us at the pier," said Kirilis. He turned to Chase. "How did you make out with Gudrun?"

"We talked a lot," said Chase.

"Talked? What's the matter, you lost your touch?"

"I think Nick is saving himself for Paola," said D'Arcy.

"Paola? Are we going to Genoa?"

"Rome wants us to recover some paintings stolen by the Germans," said Chase. "Apparently they're hidden on some island off Genoa. Szendroy will brief us on the spot. He left for Genoa by road today."

"But Genoa is in German hands."

"No more. Genoa surrendered this morning," said D'Arcy.

The limousine pulled up by the entrance to Pier 6.

"Gauchos!"

"There they are," said Kirilis.

The nurses ran up to them. "Oh, look at that," said Francesca, fondling Kirilis' cross. "Mio bravo Franco, awarded a medal."

"Ma," said Silvia, admiring Chase's.

"Hey, guys, how about pinning them?"

"Excellent idea," said Chase.

Kirilis explained the American custom of pinning.

"Oh, yes, oh, yes, I want to be pinned!" exclaimed Silvia.

"Line up," Chase told them. "Like soldiers." He waited for them to line up. "Okay, troop," he said to the Boxers. "Take your places." Each Boxer faced his woman. "Take off your medals." The Boxers took them off.

"Give a little speech," said Kirilis.

Chase took on an official tone. "For meritorious service, for hot kisses and sweet caresses, for helping out four good-for-nothing-bums to do their job, we hereby present you with the Cross of Savoy."

The Boxers pinned the medals.

"And now you pin us," said Kirilis.

The nurses took off their Red Cross pins. Francesca said, "For two very good meals, for lovely nylon stockings for sweet kisses and hot caresses . . ."

"The other way round," said Silvia.

"I mean for sweet caresses and hot kisses, we award you these pins so you will remember us when you return to America."

The girls attached the pins to the Boxers' lapels.

"And now we kiss," said Kirilis.

They kissed and ran for the Catalina. The engines of the flying boat burst to life. With a final wave to the women on the pier, the Boxers disappeared inside.

The flying boat headed for the open water, picking up speed. "Bye, bye Kramer," said Kirilis, looking out the window. He strapped his seat belt. "How long will we be in Genoa?"

"Four days," replied Chase. "We have four days in which to find those paintings. Svenson wants us back in Rome by Sunday to take a plane out on Monday."

"Where are we going?"

"Far East."

6 EXCITING ADVENTURE SERIES MEN OF ACTION BOOKS

DIRTY HARRY
by Dane Hartman
The tough, unorthodox plainclothesman of the San Francisco Police Department tackles crimes and violence—nothing can stop him.

#1 DUEL FOR CANNONS	*(C90-793, $1.95)*
#2 DEATH ON THE DOCKS	*(C90-792, $1.95)*
#3 THE LONG DEATH	*(C90-848, $1.95)*

THE HOOK
by Brad Latham
Gentleman detective, boxing legend, man-about-town, The Hook crosses 1930's America and Europe in pursuit of perpetrators of insurance fraud.

#1 THE GILDED CANARY	*(C90-882, $1.95)*
#2 SIGHT UNSEEN	*(C90-841, $1.95)*
#3 HATE IS THICKER THAN BLOOD	*(C90-986, $1.95)*

S-COM
by Steve White
High adventure with the most effective and notorious band of military mercenaries the world has known—four men and one woman with a perfect track record.

#1 THE TERROR IN TURIN	*(C90-992, $1.95)*
#2 STARS AND SWASTIKAS	*(C90-993, $1.95)*
#3 THE BATTLE IN BOTSWANA	*(C30-134, $1.95)*

BEN SLAYTON: T-MAN
by Buck Sanders
Based on actual experiences, America's most secret law-enforcement agent—the troubleshooter of the Treasury Department—combats the enemies of national security.

#1 A CLEAR AND PRESENT DANGER	*(C30-020, $1.95)*
#2 STAR OF EGYPT	*(C30-017, $1.95)*
#3 THE TRAIL OF THE TWISTED CROSS	*(C30-131, $1.95)*

NINJA MASTER
by Wade Barker
Committed to avenging injustice, Brett Wallace uses the ancient Japanese art of killing as he stalks the evildoers of the world in his mission.

#1 VENGEANCE IS HIS	*(C30-032, $1.95)*
#2 MOUNTAIN OF FEAR	*(C30-064, $1.95)*
#3 BORDERLAND OF HELL	*(C30-127, $1.95)*

BOXER UNIT—OSS
by Ned Cort
The elite 4-man commando unit of the Office of Strategic Studies whose dare-devil missions during World War II place them in the vanguard of the action.

#1 FRENCH ENTRAPMENT	*(C30-018, $1.95)*
#2 ALPINE GAMBIT	*(C30-019, $1.95)*
#3 OPERATION COUNTER-SCORCH	*(C30-128, $1.95)*